UNDERPASS

A novella by Sunanna Bhasin

© 2017

Acknowledgements

Writing this novella began with a fourth-year thesis project within the incredible Arts & Science Program at McMaster University, where I completed my undergraduate degree. I wouldn't have been able to complete this work and further improve it without the guidance and motivation provided by the following people.

A very special thanks to Dr. James King for agreeing to supervise what began as a thesis project and for all his hard work and time spent meeting with me every two weeks to edit and discuss my progress. Thank you for being an inspiring author yourself, a formidable English professor, and for believing in me.

I am also grateful Dr. Jean Wilson, for inspiring me and giving me an opportunity to write a story that means a lot to me through the Arts & Science Program. Thank you for all your teachings in our Literature class that helped me write this work.

Thank you to Anton Piatigorsky, for teaching me how to incorporate research into creative writing through our course in the Arts & Science Program, and for being an inspirational figure in my writing career. Thank you for encouraging me not to give up.

Lastly, a huge thank you to my family for supporting my writing.

Dedicated to my family

PART I: ASHA KAUR

Chapter 1

Asha Kaur sat in silence as her husband turned on the ignition of his spotless white Range Rover, the latest model, of course. He would never buy anything even remotely out-dated because Jitendra Jha was a classy high roller, or so he liked to think. Although his daughter on many occasions would scoldingly point out what a squanderer he could be, even she had grown accustomed to his extravagant ways of living. In fact, one of the things she enjoyed most was taking her father's Range Rover for long drives in the suburban countryside so that she could have some time to herself, away from her parents' fighting on some days, escaping her father's endless alcohol consumption on most nights. There was something captivating about driving along endless straight roads, right into the sunset. The hypnotic pinks and yellows of the sun going down in tandem with that perfect summer evening breeze – warm enough to keep the window all the way down, but cool enough to scrap the A/C. The music just right, some blend of alt-rock and mellow indie pop, or perhaps the classic French ballad, and the light winds blowing through her hair giving her the soft tousled waves she tends to battle with using a straightener when she goes out. It was those car rides that were liberating, but also necessary. Sometimes the escapism she needed couldn't come from a Netflix drama. Sometimes she just needed the entrancing drive surrounded by green fields and open road. Deepika almost felt guilty when she was bidding her parents goodbye after they had dropped her off at her residence in downtown Toronto. In that moment, she had felt as though she would miss her father's beautiful car more than she would miss him. It was an internal conflict that she couldn't always understand, but it existed and it both freed her and saddened her. It was not as though Jitendra was completely unaware of his daughter's mixed feelings towards him, but he also knew that she loved him deeply. After all, why would she try so hard to save him from himself if she didn't care in the first place?

Asha knew that she wouldn't see her daughter for a while now, not until Thanksgiving most likely. Deepika had never promised her parents that she'd return earlier, but now that it was her final year of her undergraduate studies at the University of Toronto, they were used to her schedule. Both Asha and Jitendra understood her choice to refrain from visiting often during the school year. Not only was she busy with the program, she was so enamoured by it, that she had managed to secure a short-term teaching assistant position with her comparative literature professor. As an undergraduate, that was not easy to accomplish. Asha was well aware of this, as she too, had been in love with English but was unable to pursue it due to her father's wishes. It was for this reason that she and Jitendra never pushed Deepika in any one direction.

As Jitendra merged onto the highway, Asha gripped the passenger door's handle and shut her eyes tightly. She hated travelling at high speeds, particularly in cars, and more particularly in the evening. Thankfully, because it was just the beginning of September – September 7, 2016 – the nights were relatively long and the sun didn't go down until around 8:00 PM in the evening. They had been cruising at a steady speed for about ten minutes, so Asha was finally able to relax. She dabbed at the tiny beads of sweat that had coated her forehead with a leftover napkin she had crumpled up in her pocket discreetly enough for Jitendra not to notice. She didn't necessarily have anything to say at the moment and didn't feel like saying he was okay when there was so much on her mind that made her feel like she wasn't. As if he had heard her thoughts, Jitendra reached for the volume control and within seconds, the soothing sounds of jazz filled the car. The sentimental piano took Asha to another time, before she had ever met Jitendra, before she had been forced to grow up as fast as she had.

Asha was propped up on her not-so-comfortable single bed, lying on her stomach with her legs dangling in the air in her modest hostel room (she liked to think it was quite cozy). She was engrossed by an especially heated scene in her fifth Harlequin romance novel of the week. These sorts of books were not allowed at the New Delhi Catholic high school she attended with her best friend, Priya Singh. These sorts of books were sinful and dirty. Asha laughed as she remembered one of the headmistresses commenting on how filthy the novels were after skimming the page Asha had been reading in the middle of class. Of course, she just had to interrupt Asha's reading of an exceptionally erotic scene, which frankly, was Asha's first time reading such carnal descriptions. *I'll bet you she's dying to finish that book. Poor woman hasn't been laid in years,* Priya had commented devilishly on their way back home from school. The memory caused Asha to burst into another fit of laughter. Shaking her head smiling, as she remembered how the headmistress's face had turned a magnificent beet red, she flipped the pages in utter suspense, longing to find out whether the female protagonist would be kissed by the tall, dark, and handsome mystery man. She swung her legs in excitement as she blazed through the text, dying to know the young girl's fate.

"Oy, Ash!" the dorm room's door flew open and there stood the one and only Priya Singh radiating confidence with her arms full of Asha's favourite Haldirams namkeen – savoury Indian snacks packed with calories and bliss. Priya was the biggest extrovert Asha knew, aside from herself. She would approach a complete stranger and ask him to bed if she thought he was attractive enough. She was a whole new level of 'paagal', Asha would tell her almost every day, as she would be up to her crazy antics 24/7. Priya had medium-length dark brown hair and large eyes full of wonder and excitement. She was relatively lean in comparison to Asha, probably because she would bring packets upon packets of Haldirams to their hostel and give them to all her friends but only eat a spoonful herself!

Asha, looking pointedly annoyed, glanced up from her novel. She disliked being interrupted in the middle of reading. It felt as though she had been transported to another world and then plucked from it. When she saw her best friend standing in the doorway with her favourite kind of munchies, her eyes softened and she couldn't help but feel her heart warm.

"Arey, kya hai?" Asha attempted to sound displeased with her friend, but her lips turned up in a smile as soon as she saw Priya glance at the novel in her hands and roll her eyes.

"You know what, Ash? I shouldn't even be surprised that you're reading this Romeo Shomeo nonsense again," she joked and her Indian accent came through strongly. Kicking the door behind her, she tossed the snacks onto her bed. She sat on the edge of her bed and faced her friend.

Asha put her book away and sighed, "I can't believe this is our last year of high school. It feels like yesterday that I met you, do you remember that?"

Priya burst into laughter, "How could I forget? Your expression was priceless!"

3

"Yeah, probably because I wasn't expecting to be greeted by a random couple snogging in my dorm room, idiot!" Asha slapped her friend's shoulder playfully, reminiscing about all the hilarious memories they had shared, "What was that boy's name again?"

Priya finally stopped laughing and replied, "Akshay. Akshay Kapoor. He was hot, yaar."

"You're insane, Priya. Hey, have you figured out college applications yet?" Asha's mind drifted to the many university applications she was in the middle of. She and Priya had planned to work on them together since grade eleven.

"Oh please Ash, it's only the beginning of senior year. We'll do them next month, I promise. Part of me is just putting it off because I don't want to leave yet. Where are we going to end up? It's a bit terrifying, don't you think?" Priya paused briefly and then added, "The other part of me is just apathetic if I'm being straight-up about it."

She spoke so seriously about her laziness that Asha laughed initially. Then, she thought about where they were going and didn't know how to feel, "I don't know – I just wish Papa would be more accepting of the fact that English is my passion, and science is just something I'm good at. He doesn't understand that. I mean studying English makes my heart race. It's not the same feeling when I'm reading about the sciences."

Priya hopped off the bed and stalked across the room with her arms out to her sides and a stern expression on her face, "Asha Kaur! English?! Have you lost your mind, beta? I am a world-renowned heart surgeon and will be able to get you into the best hospitals in India. Don't tell me you want to study this – this, useless literature!" Priya stormed over to Asha with a large frown on her face and her lower lip jutting out to imitate Mr. Kaur's typical demeanour when he was angry. She grabbed the Harlequin romance novel off the side table and held it in the air and shook it before shouting, "Absolutely, not!"

At this point Asha was on the floor in hysterics. This was exactly why Priya was her best friend because even during a serious conversation about their future, she could make her laugh and forget that it bothered her so much to begin with. Priya joined Asha on the floor and they spent a good ten minutes giggling about how severe

Mr. Kaur could be in his overall disposition the minute a word was said against the sciences and in favour of the liberal arts.

Asha snapped out of her reverie when Jitendra asked her if she was okay. She just looked at him and nodded. He drummed his fingers against the steering wheel and knitted his eyebrows, as though he was struggling to string a coherent sentence together, but quickly decided not to speak instead. They were silent once again, and the only conversation that was taking place in the car was between a saxophone and a trumpet. The two instruments were imitating each other, running after each other, each trying so hard to keep up but inevitably one was always a couple of notes ahead. They'd end on the same note though. These sorts of pieces always end on a pure whole note. The couple was just half an hour away from their home in North York when the radio announcer's voice replaced the charming melody to state the artist and album, to which Jitendra gave a subtle nod. Asha wasn't paying much attention to the radio, however. She simply couldn't help but smile to herself as she recalled the amount of silliness she and Priya had participated in during their years in high school and even college. They had gone to the same one, the University of Delhi. Deepika was truly following in her footsteps except for the fact that she had the liberty to study what she enjoyed. One of the biggest things Asha loved about Jitendra was that he, too, encouraged Deepika to pursue her passions, and that didn't necessarily mean just English. It was whatever she wanted. She didn't owe them an explanation, she wasn't expected to present a list of pros and cons. The only expectation they had for her was that she complete her university degree and do well. Yet, Deepika had been quite vocal about the fact that English literature was the one subject that made her heart flutter, that incited a combination of nerves and thrill within her. *It makes my heart race.* Asha remembered what she had told Priya that day in their hostel and knew that if it was the same feeling Deepika had about literature – if it made her feel alive – then she would be a selfish parent to discourage her from pursuing it. So she never did. She would support her daughter all the way through.

"It's amazing how much success Dee has had at U of T in as little as three years," Jitendra spoke up after almost an hour of quiet. It was as though he had read Asha's mind. Despite their differences, sometimes she was astonished at the depth of their emotional connection. Perhaps that was why she could never bring herself to leave him, even when he had given her many reasons to do so. Maybe she was weak, or maybe just one good reason to stay was enough. Loving him that deeply meant that a single reason, or multiple smaller reasons, was all she needed to reassure her that he was worth it. Asha turned to look at her husband and for the first time, noticed just how much he had aged. His short once jet-black hair, still parted to the right side, had grown largely grey. The salt-and-pepper colouring was visible in his beard as well, but it was the fatigue in his eyes that struck her the most. It looked like he hadn't slept for days. Asha knew why. He was trying his hardest not to drink. He had been trying for a week. Midway, he had succumbed to the Chardonnay given by a close friend as a thank-you for setting him up with a client. However, for at least four days, he had been completely sober. While Asha and Deepika were proud of him, they were also concerned. This wasn't something he should be doing without professional help. Thankfully, it wouldn't be long before he got some, so Asha relaxed and briefly placed her hand over the one he had resting on the gearshift.

"Yes, it is. Jeet, I am sure she will be more successful than either of us could imagine," Asha smiled and retracted her short, yet reassuring touch. Thinking about where they were headed and how they had gotten to this point made her realize that their 21-year old daughter was about to graduate from university and begin her own life without knowing what made Asha who she was. Every year on her birthday, Deepika would write a piece for Asha, whether it was a poem or a card, something to let her know how much she appreciated her mother. Asha knew everything about Deepika, but lately, she felt that Deepika had distanced herself from the family. She was growing into herself, making her own life, and perhaps because Asha was so used to Deepika's frequent concern, less of it made her seem withdrawn. The reality was that Asha had always wanted her daughter to find her own way because that freedom was the one thing she never completely had.

She looked back at Jitendra, who was entirely focused on the road. She wondered what was going through his mind. He hardly shared his thoughts without alcohol there to open him up. For something that tends to make so many people go numb, it surely did

6

not have the same effect on him. It opened him up, the same way an aged wine goes from tart to bright and smooth after being left to settle nicely in an untouched glass. Although Jitendra didn't turn out to be the man that Asha initially thought he would be, it wasn't that she didn't love him. It was that she had learned to love him despite initially feeling like she had from the start. Indian marriages at her time often unfolded that way. She leaned against the car window and passed her fingers through her greying raven-coloured hair and closed her eyes in meditation. They would be home soon.

Chapter 2

"Asha!" Indu Kaur called her daughter. They were about to meet another potential match. Asha had no interest whatsoever in getting married at the ripe age of 24, "Asha! Woh aya hai!" He was here. The next man she would reject.

Her mother was by no means forcing her to get married, but the family was a bit concerned that she still hadn't met someone. After all, if grandchildren were to be part of the picture, they would have to think about marriage sooner rather than later. Asha still couldn't understand why these suitors were responding to the picture and description she had put out. She purposely had Priya take a particularly unflattering shot of her, wherein she looked more like Frankenstein's monster's bride-to-be than anything else. Surely, these men didn't like frizzy oily brown hair shooting in every possible direction – and Asha was sure she hadn't washed it that day – nor the unsmiling, unenthusiastic version of her that she reserved for them. And if they did, well, Asha was petrified at the prospect of what they may look like! Despite all that effort, week after week, a new man was interested in courting her, and week after week, she would smile, ask him difficult questions, and walk away. Indu didn't particularly like any of the boys that had shown interest so far, so she didn't force her daughter to make a hasty decision. For one, their manner of speaking was horrendously off. They had some strange superiority complex, likely fostered by their parents' beliefs that they were meant for extraordinary things simply because they were Indian men. Secondly, Indu could see that Asha was either not attracted to them enough to see them again or that her daughter was thoroughly repulsed by both their words and outward appearances. Yet, she'd hope that each time she invited another suitor over that there would at least be a spark between Asha and the incredibly lucky man.

Asha huffed loudly from her bedroom, collected herself and walked gracefully into the living room. Upon entering, she was pleasantly surprised to be greeted by her parents' close friends. When her father was alive, he had met Raj and Anjali Mehta in elementary school. They had remained friends ever since, and naturally, the friendship became familial as it often does when one member is so involved. Asha adored the Mehtas. They were practically family, so she thought of them as aunt and uncle, and they had claimed her as their niece. A significant part of her childhood was spent in their care when her mother was busy working part-time in administration and her father's job at the hospital meant unpredictable hours and many long days. She was so happy to see them that she did not notice the three extra pairs of shoes neatly placed on the mat by the front door. Her tense eyebrows immediately relaxed when Mrs. Mehta opened her arms to receive her. The frown she had intended to wear to scare off the suitor disappeared the second Mrs. Mehta asked her how she was doing in teacher's college.

"I can't tell you how much I enjoy it, Anjali Aunty," Asha beamed, still embracing her favourite aunt, "I adore working with young children, more than I thought I would."

Mr. Mehta chuckled at Asha's enthusiasm, "See, Asha, teaching science isn't as bad as you thought it would be!"

Asha shook her head contentedly and bowed slightly so that she could touch Mr. Mehta's feet. Although it was a common Indian practice to touch elders' feet as a form of respectful greeting, or *pranama*, Asha's family had never really embraced that cultural aspect of India. Asha herself didn't like the concept of bowing down to anyone. She'd always preferred a handshake or a hug because she'd like to think her relationships could be level – that she and her elder could be on equal footing. It didn't surprise Asha, then, when her uncle stopped her before she could complete the gesture and gave her a tight hug instead.

"Come on, I'm no stranger, beta," Mr. Mehta joked.

Raj Mehta was a biology professor, an atheist, and highly critical of many Indian customs on the basis of their being favourable towards men. He was always vocal about his views and logic at family dinner parties, and Asha admired him for that. She emulated that part of him when she could. The person who tried to keep her quiet and submissive would have to answer directly to hell, she thought. Asha had a particular affinity towards the Mehtas because of their non-traditional views and the fact that they were willing to engage in controversial discussion on almost any topic. Her father, Kartik Kaur, had been more conventional giving rise to many arguments between father and daughter. Thankfully, Asha had her progressive mother, Indu, and the Mehtas to back her on any

10

"non-ideal" notion she'd held, according to her father. Asha had always thought that she would have had to fight with her father over the fact that she was unwilling to take her future husband's surname. However, after his death, her wish was not met with much resistance. Her uncle played a big role in convincing her mother that it was completely acceptable, after all, *let the boy take the girl's name after all she is sacrificing for him*! She couldn't forget her uncle's words when Indu was initially surprised at Asha's perspective on it. He was right. An Indian woman was expected to leave her family home for a man who would likely be a total stranger, and then to ask her to change her name, something Asha saw as a large part of her identity, well that was borderline ludicrous! Indu hadn't been difficult to persuade, but some of the suitors that had come to see Asha so far were a bit taken aback at the request. If such a simple and sensible idea was a deal-breaker, then Asha had no desire to marry such a man. That sort of man turned her off immediately because that sort of man seemed to her to want ownership, to claim her. She wanted a partner, a teammate, not a king to worship.

Asha let go of her dear uncle and said, "It's so good to see you, Raj Uncle."

"Just as it is always wonderful to see you thriving, Asha. I am so glad to hear how well you are doing in teacher's college. How is Priya doing?"

Asha couldn't help but smile when she thought of her best friend, "Oh, she is doing very well, Raj Uncle. She's doing finance-related stuff – honestly, I'm not sure exactly what it is. Business was never my forte!"

Both Indu and the Mehtas laughed in unison. They all knew Priya Singh very well because she would come over almost every day when Asha was in college.

"Asha," Indu began, after the laughter had quieted, "the reason Raj Uncle and Anjali Aunty are here is because they want you to meet their friends' son, Jitendra."

Asha's smile faded slightly. Of course there was a catch. Could she not just enjoy her relatives' company without a man interfering with her fun? Still, she tried her best to be polite because it was the Mehtas who were friends with this family. If they were anything alike, Asha knew she would be in good hands.

She followed her mother with long strides and her head held high into the living room. She refused to give off a reserved persona just to make this Jitendra character feel more comfortable. Despite her initial feelings, her scepticism began to wear off when she saw him sitting on the couch next to his mother and father donning a white dinner jacket and dark blue denim jeans. He had on one of the most inviting smiles she had ever seen and his sharp sense of style made him even more attractive to her.

"Asha, this is Mr. Dev Jha and Mrs. Archana Jha," Anjali introduced her friends. Asha bent down to touch their feet, but even they interrupted her midway and gave her their blessings happily.

Asha smiled at them and glanced to the left of them when she saw Jitendra stand up. He had sharp features but his expression was soft – the hint of a smile remained on his lips. He ran his fingers through his raven-coloured hair that was parted somewhat carelessly to one side. She liked that he hadn't slicked back his hair or worn a full business suit complemented with a briefcase and notebook like some of the previous men had. She liked that he wasn't so calculated and clean. There was something genuine about the way he hadn't shaved the little bit of scruff covering both cheeks and that despite the fact that his naturally wavy hair was fighting the way it had been parted, he still hadn't used an atrocious amount of gel to slick it back.

"Asha, this is our son Jitendra," Mrs. Jha spoke softly, moving out of the way so that Jitendra could extend his hand and introduce himself to Asha.

"Call me Jeet," he grinned as Asha took his hand. Her confidence from earlier on wavered slightly due to a sudden rush of passion for this man whom she did not know. Perhaps it was his distinguished style and mysterious nature that intrigued her so, or perhaps she needed to take Priya's advice and stop reading those ridiculous Harlequin romances! She stifled a laugh when she heard her friend's voice in her head and composed herself before responding.

"It's nice to meet you, Jeet," Asha said just before letting go of his hand, "I'd say you can call me Ash, but you have to get to know me first." Asha surprised herself with her flirtatious comment, and both Indu and Anjali chuckled softly.

"I look forward to it," Jeet smiled and gestured for everyone to sit back down on the couch. He had a leader-like air about him, Asha thought. He had only spoken a few words, but she could read much more in his mannerisms. He appeared to be the kind of person that walks into a room and grabs everyone's attention, the life of the party.

While the families conversed, she found out that Jeet was a businessman, like his father. He had started his own IT business in which he would provide technical support to various clients, both large and small companies. When she heard that he hadn't attended college, she was a bit surprised. He came across as quite well read and interesting, and he was. He enjoyed reading just about everything, from the news to historical fiction, he said.

"What made you decide not to pursue post-secondary education?" Asha asked, a little disappointed. She'd been fixated on that since he mentioned it. Given the amount of education she had completed, she had deemed it a requirement for her future partner. She couldn't deny its value, but she might have to make an exception for Jeet. She could feel her principles blurring in her mind. There was something about this man that made her feel like her ideals may have been too much, that maybe he could make her happy even though he didn't meet her list of requirements. The room was quiet after Asha's question, and she instantly regretted asking.

After a few seconds of uncomfortable silence, Jitendra spoke up, but made his statement quick, "I took the wrong advice." Everyone could tell that he wasn't willing to talk about it further, but Asha was impressed with his placid response, seeing as this was clearly a sensitive topic for him. That was probably the toughest question she had asked him that afternoon. After the brief awkward period, the conversation went quite smoothly. Asha learned that Jitendra had two younger sisters, Anita and Gauri, who both lived in Chandigarh, their birthplace. Asha had heard of the Jha family before their meeting, in a different context of course, so she was not shocked to find out that Jitendra lived and worked out of Canada. She wasn't sure if she would be able to leave her mother behind in India if this was a good match. While the thought scared her, she knew that her mother must have known that this was a possibility before she agreed to let the Mehtas introduce Jitendra to her. It was much too early to be thinking of marriage, though. This was a preliminary meeting, just a first date really. What Asha would have liked to do was meet Jitendra once without the parents around so that she could really get to know him. They spent too much time asking about technicalities – his work, the hours, income, housing – of course that was important, but Asha would much rather get a sense of his personality, habits, and hobbies, what made *his* heart race and flutter, before even approaching the notion of marriage.

"Can I see you again?" Jitendra interrupted Asha's thoughts, holding his hand out once more as his parents stood up ready to leave. Asha blushed at his sweet demeanour. He *was* charming all right.

She shook his hand slowly but firmly. Her father had taught her always to give a firm handshake to display confidence: *Never falter in your handshake. Never demonstrate that you are less than an equal.*

"That would be very nice," Asha smiled, still thinking of how much nicer it would be if they could go out somewhere instead.

It was as though Jeet had read her mind because he smirked just before leaning into her so he could whisper, "Perhaps without our families, next time."

Asha felt her cheeks heat up when Jeet got close to her but she remained as calm as possible and waved goodbye to the Jha family as they walked out the front door. Jeet was the last to leave. He stole a quick glance back at Asha before exiting, and upon seeing that her family wasn't paying attention, he shot her a playful wink and grinned as he turned to shut the front door behind him.

Asha jolted into the present and out of her daydream when Jeet returned to the kitchen after shutting the patio door a bit too harshly. Life happens fast, she thought. Meeting him was still such a vivid memory, and now she was living with him, loving him, tolerating him, forgiving him, and then loving him some more. She stood up and turned the kettle on again because the water she had intended to boil for her tea had already cooled while she had been pondering the past at the circular table in the centre of the kitchen. After leaving the barbecued chicken on the counter and quietly letting Asha know that it was done, Jeet left the room hastily and propped himself in front of the television to watch the baseball game. Asha hardly had a second to acknowledge his efforts because he retreated to his favourite spot in the house so quickly. She glanced at the counter by the dinner table and saw a brand new bottle of vodka sitting there tantalizingly, unopened. He must have taken it out yesterday and then changed his mind. She realized why he didn't want to linger in the kitchen – it would simply prompt him to fall into his nightly ritual of grabbing a crystal glass from the cabinet. The clink of the glass, the ice machine working effortfully, the sound of the ice cracking as the alcohol caresses its endless surfaces. She was too used to those painful sounds. Asha grabbed the bottle and hid it in the garage under a shelf to minimize her husband's temptations.

While Jeet was watching the game, Asha prepared some salad and logged into her email. A flood of happiness washed over her when she saw a new email from Deepika with the subject line: AMAZING NEWS. That is just what she needed at the moment. She was exhausted from the events of the past couple of weeks, but her daughter's email after just one day of separation rejuvenated her worn out spirit. She opened the email and learned that Deepika had been accepted to participate in an incredible opportunity to complete part of her final year in the French Riviera with her studies focusing on French literature. Asha was ecstatic for her daughter because she had been confident that with her stellar grades and diverse extracurricular activities, Deepika would undoubtedly receive an offer of admission. Asha called out to Jeet from the kitchen and asked if he had received Deepika's email. It turned out that she had cc'd him, contrary to what Asha had expected. Jeet walked into the kitchen smiling and stood behind Asha as she read the rest of the message. He squeezed her shoulders affectionately and said softly, "I knew she'd do great things."

Chapter 3

It was Saturday morning. Asha had just finished a cup of her favourite Earl Grey tea and was sitting on the patio with Jitendra listening to the soothing melodies of Nina Simone. Jitendra was reading the paper while Asha was engrossed in her Reader's Digest. She was in the middle of a piece of poetry about estrangement when she came across a photograph she had placed between the pages so as to remember to put it in its appropriate place. It was a picture of Deepika writing a letter to her grandmother after having graduated high school. Asha wiped a solitary tear from her eye as she remembered how excited Indu had been to receive the letter back in India.

Asha missed her mother on many special occasions, but thankfully they spoke on the phone a few times a week to catch up. Deepika had been so busy at school lately that simply receiving a brief email made Asha happy. She had tried to call her daughter at school but often got voicemail and an apologetic text a few hours later stating that her phone had been on silent or that she had been out with friends. Asha looked at the photograph in her hands again. Her daughter loved to read and write, as did she, but she hadn't written anything of substance in a while. A thought came to her as she went up to her bedroom to add the photo to her album: she would write letters to Deepika. Deepika had blamed Asha for staying with Jitendra despite himself without really understanding why she made that decision. The reality was that her daughter didn't know as much about her as she should, Asha frowned. The best way for her to convey this was through a medium her daughter could appreciate. Asha sat down at her antique mahogany writing desk and pulled a few sheets of off-white vintage paper from the drawer. Her fingers naturally ran over the crisp surfaces of the specialty letter paper she had purchased a while back. She opened the second drawer slowly to reveal her modest collection of fountain pens she had kept safe for years. She picked her favourite one – a Parker 75, sterling silver with a beautiful cross-etched pattern. *That pattern's called 'Cisele' in French*, Deepika had commented a few months ago when admiring Asha's collection.

Asha planned to give this pen to her daughter for her graduation ever since she saw the excitement in her eyes when she had first held it – it was the same elation she had felt when her father had bought it for her to write her poetry when she was a teenager. Her father had no idea how much poetry his sudden death had inspired. Asha had pages upon pages of it – she had found a way to translate grief and loss into words. It was a great talent to have - and she saw it in Deepika - this ability to take an unfathomable emotion and make it into something tangible. Asha smiled to herself as she thought of how similar she and her daughter truly were.

She peered into her drawer once more and ruffled through the sheets of crumpled poetry she had kept from her youth. *Why had she ever stopped writing*, she thought confusedly. She shook her head and focused her attention on the paper in front of her. She had so much to say that she didn't know where to start. Taking a deep breath, she smoothed the edges of the paper with her thumbs, positioned the nib of her pen in the top left corner of the page, and put her swirling thoughts to paper.

Dear Dee,

I can't tell you how proud I am of all your accomplishments. You have done what I have always dreamed of, so I hope you don't mind your mother living vicariously through you! Jokes aside, I wanted you to know that no matter how you may feel about your father given recent events, that both of us are here for you. You should know just how much he loves you. He is so delighted with your achievements at school. I wish you could see how animated he gets when he reads your emails. Sometimes he even reads them aloud, can you imagine that? You know him well, Deepika. He's not the best at communicating his feelings, but he lets me in more often than you think. I'm not saying that he hasn't made a big mistake, and I'm not trying to make you forget what he's done. In fact, promise me you never will, so that you never confound what is right and what is wrong.

You must find it difficult to understand how I remain by your father's side after this major offence. Forgive me for not being a stronger person in your eyes – it is my one regret. However, when you love someone as much as I love your father, and I know you love him too, you don't make excuses for them. You support them for as long as you can. I know that we've had disagreements on this topic, and I am sorry for getting upset with you. The truth is, my parents fought in front of me as well, and the number of times I begged my mother to leave my father…believe me, I understand your frustration. But, Dee, there is so much I feel I haven't shared with you, and I want to. You're growing up, and you're going to meet people from all walks of life. Some of them will scare you because you've met them before, and others, will challenge everything you've ever believed in. That's why you have to be sure of yourself. I already see a confidence in you that took me much longer to attain. I know I hardly speak about my own father, but it's only to protect you. Like your father, he became a heavy drinker. I have been trying to come to terms with what happened to him – how he completely destroyed himself – but every day I see him in your father and I can't move on. I couldn't save my father, but maybe I can save my husband.

Asha's hand shook as she scribbled the last few words down. Her left hand reflexively shot up to wipe her tears before they could run down her cheeks. She loosened her grip and let her pen fall. If she didn't try to calm down, she would lose control and her sporadic anxiety would get the best of her. Gazing at the ceiling, she allowed her entire body to relax and concentrated on her breathing.

"Asha, what nonsense is this?!" Kartik Kaur's deep booming voice filled the constricted spaces between the drab walls of the New Delhi DLF apartment complex his family lived in.

The 16-year old girl entered the tiny living room where her father sat crouched over a sheet of paper and her mother was trying her best to calm him. Asha's head was bowed slightly as she twiddled her thumbs nervously when she approached her parents. She had received her first science test marks for the tenth standard.

"I'm sorry, Papa," Asha said quietly. She wasn't one to be scared easily, but her father was unrelenting in his anger when it came to her schoolwork. She knew that his strong reaction was for her sake, but she also felt as though he was unfairly harsh. Last week, she had been awarded an A on a major English paper worth almost half her overall mark for the course, and while her mother was ecstatic and called Priya over for dinner to celebrate, all she got from her father was a slight nod and a 'good'.

"What did I tell you about spending too much time writing that flowery poetry and whatnot? Had you spent more time studying for this test, you would have done well," Kartik's voice had softened

19

upon seeing his daughter's regret, but he remained firm.

"I know, I am sorry. It won't happen again," Asha replied, lifting her head so that her eyes could meet her father's. The darkness within them had faded and he smiled faintly.

"It's okay, beta. I only get upset because I know you can do much better. If I had no hope for you, I wouldn't say a word."

"I know, Papa. I'll go do my homework now, if that's okay," Asha looked at her parents for approval. Indu smiled at her knowingly because both of them had learned how to please the often-overbearing Kartik Kaur. He hadn't seen the subtle exchange between mother and daughter. Then again, he hardly ever did. He simply nodded and asked Indu to get him a glass of whiskey on ice – the usual for a Thursday night, Friday night, the weekend of course…the usual. Asha left the living room happily. If there was one positive thing about her father's addiction, it was that he inspired so much of her writing. She knew that she would have to do better on her next science test. Her mark wasn't even acceptable for her standards, yet she wasn't about to give up her weekly ritual of speedwriting with Priya.

If her father didn't allow Priya to come over, they would do it over the phone. Priya would blast music on her Boombox to time their sessions. Their favourite track to write to was "Keep on Loving You" by REO Speedwagon. In many cases, they would finish writing their pieces and then replay the song so that they could do a sing-along over the phone. If they were together in Asha's bedroom, Indu would often walk in on them dancing to Olivia Newton-John's "Physical" on Asha's bed and would proceed to scold them laughingly after giving them hot parathas and yogurt to eat.

Kartik was hardly privy to these activities. In fact, Asha would be surprised if he were able to name one of her favourite English songs. No one blamed him. Being one of New Delhi's best heart surgeons was an exhausting job. Asha tended to look on the positives of his regular absence during the day and often at dinner. For one, she could write to her heart's content. The other plus was that she could have Priya and her mother over. There were frequent girls' nights at DLF, and Asha didn't mind it. After all, it was much better than watching her father drink himself to sleep each night. How he managed to get up at 5 A.M. every morning and perform the most complex surgeries bewildered her, but she did not bother trying to comprehend it. After all, understanding him as a person was difficult enough for her; there was no way she would be able to decipher the logic behind his habits.

Asha sighed as she thought of her father. She missed him terribly because despite his flaws, he had loved her and had shown it, in his own way. It was a way of showing love that a child would not understand. She'd had to grow up to understand his kind of love, the kind that wasn't evident in his words. It was the kind of love that could only be seen in what was not said. She almost had to imagine it as a child because it seemed so twisted that shouting and coarseness could be her father's way of demonstrating affection. She recognized his mannerisms and his ways and vowed that she would never let her own child feel like he or she needed to guess if they were loved. Not if she could help it. She drummed her fingers on her desk and debated whether she should write more to Deepika or go for a walk. When her daughter stayed with them during the summers, they would go for hour-long walks daily. They were more for chatting than for the exercise. Sometimes they would return happier than before, and on the odd occasion, angrier.

Asha smiled to herself and decided that she could use the fresh air. She wasn't sure how to proceed with the letter because she was still battling her own demons regarding her father. There was no way for her to overcome it unless she talked about what happened, so she made a determined decision to reveal more. She had to. She had kept her emotions bottled up for much too long. At least when she used to write poetry, there was some form of catharsis. Lately, however, her energy was spent taking care of and worrying for Jeet. *Perhaps her own fatal flaw was that she cared too much for people who couldn't bother about themselves*, she pondered to herself. It was a knee-jerk reaction, to forgo her own well being to help someone struggling. As much as Deepika had told her to distance herself from Jeet so that he could see what he would lose if he kept up his awful behaviour, the second she felt he was alone, she would be there.

Chapter 4

"What on earth is the matter, Kartik?" Indu ran after him when he stormed into their apartment, furiously tossed his brand new black leather briefcase onto the couch and strode into his bedroom. He slammed the door hard enough to let Indu know that he was not in the mood to be disturbed.

Indu could not understand what prompted his sudden return from work and why he seemed so angry. Still, she knew him well enough to know that speaking to him now would only throw him into a deeper rage. She decided that she wouldn't worry about it and began preparing their dinner. In the morning Kartik had been in such a good mood that he had specially requested she make his favourite vegetarian dish – shalgam ki sabzi. It was a spicy turnip curry that he enjoyed eating every now and then. He liked to eat it with a crispy hot roti right off the cast iron pan. Indu smiled as she remembered how his face would light up upon seeing his favourite dish on the table after coming home from a long day of work. His inexplicable demeanour concerned her, but the only things in her control at the moment were the stove in front of her and the ingredients she would fuse together to make her husband's day better. She kept herself busy for a good hour and tried to push the prodding thought that something horrible had happened at the hospital to the back of her mind.

The food was ready. Kartik still hadn't come out of their room. Indu stood by the stove and mindlessly wiped her hands with a dirty hand towel. Her eyes were fixed on the bedroom door, which she could see was unquestionably shut to keep her out rather than keep him in. Had she not been home, she was sure he would be pouring himself a glass – probably more if things had not gone well at work. She let out a frustrated exhale when she saw that her hands were dirtier than before and shook her head at her absent-mindedness as she rinsed her hands in the sink. Half an hour later, the table had been laid and Indu was sitting with a copy of Albert Camus' *The Stranger*, which Asha had given her excitedly, exclaiming that she absolutely must read it when she had the chance. Indu was glad that Asha was staying over at Priya's house that night because her daughter would have felt bad if Kartik didn't eat with them the one night that he was back in time for dinner. Even two hours later, Indu's plate remained untouched. She was hoping Kartik would tell her what was going on, or at least eat with her, but as the clock struck 10 P.M., she began to lose confidence in both possibilities. She wasn't about to starve herself, so she proceeded to eat the lukewarm meal without bothering to reheat it. She was much too tired. Before retreating to her room, she covered Kartik's plate and left it out for him in case he was waiting for her to sleep so he could eat alone. She was right.

When she had entered their bedroom, she found Kartik lying on his side in his medical coat, dress shirt, and pants facing the wall with his eyes closed. He hadn't even taken his belt or watch off. His stethoscope had been carelessly tossed on the floor, although he had probably intended for it to land on the chair and had been too exhausted to move it. She moved quietly in the room, changed into her nightclothes, and making every effort not to disturb him, even though she knew he was simply waiting for her to fall asleep, she got into bed and lay on her side facing away from him. Pretending to have fallen asleep, just as he had, Indu felt the mattress shift as Kartik got up and left the room making little noise as he shut the door behind him.

In the kitchen, Kartik couldn't help but smile when he saw the plate Indu had made for him. He put it in the microwave and while he waited for it to heat up, he poured himself a shot of straight whiskey. He had drunk three shots in the two minutes he had been waiting for his dinner. When the food was done heating up, he poured himself a glass of scotch on ice and diluted it with water. He walked over to the couch by the television set and placed his meal on the coffee table just before turning the TV on to some miscellaneous news channel.

When he stood up to take his lab coat off, he caught a glimpse of his reflection in the decorative mirror on the wall just as he tossed the coat onto the rocking chair by the couch. His eyes were red thanks to a combination of his crying and drinking. Of course, his wife would have attributed his unkempt appearance solely to the alcohol, and that was fine with him. He'd rather she keep believing that than find out what had really happened. Of course, he would have to tell his wife and daughter eventually because someone or the other would certainly make them aware of the situation even if he remained silent. News spread quickly among families in India. This was the result of too many tea parties and an abundance of time among the upper class. The news spread even more quickly when you were one of the most well-known surgeons in the region. To be renowned for performing life-saving surgeries exceptionally well was an honour. But to be known for being inebriated while a patient's life lay in your unsteady hands, well, that was utter humiliation. Kartik rubbed his temples with his hands. He had never acknowledged that he had a problem with alcohol up until this point in his life. The hospital had fired him because of his unprofessional behaviour, but his saving grace was that he had reproached himself more severely than they did. *How could he have taken such a risk with someone's life,* he wanted someone to beat him for being so selfish. The guilt was consuming him, and the alcohol was too. The only difference was that the former would keep him up at night while the latter would at least knock him out hard enough to make today's problems disappear for a brief time.

The next morning, Indu was up at 6 A.M. She had hardly slept. At midnight, she had accepted the fact that Kartik was probably passed out on the couch in the living room. She had stopped herself from retrieving a blanket from the closet and placing it over him for fear that she would catch him awake. Still, she hadn't slept a wink. Upon entering the kitchen, she saw Kartik as she had expected to see him. Yet, even her anticipation of his state could not prepare her fully. As she approached the couch to lift the half-finished glass of scotch from his clutch – how he had managed to keep his grip tight enough while sleeping so as not to spill it was beyond her – she saw that he looked a good five years older than he had prior to last night.

There were prominent bags under his eyes. His disheveled hair looked greyer that morning, and the veins in his hands, which were crossed over his chest as he slept, seemed to bulge more than usual. *He needs to wake up and clean himself up before Asha gets home*, Indu thought. She didn't want her daughter to come home to her passed out father after having a lovely time with her friend. Just as she was about to wake Kartik, the kitchen phone rang. At this early hour, it was either the hospital or a family emergency. Little did Indu know that it could be both.

"Hello," Indu spoke into the receiver softly, watching Kartik as he stirred slightly and then fell back into unconsciousness.

Less than five minutes later, Indu was off the phone. She was in shock. It had been the hospital. They had told her that Kartik had been suspended from practicing indefinitely and that he needed to come pick up some of his belongings. She hadn't been able to believe a single word they were telling her. After all these years, what could he have possibly done wrong? *He had been under the influence during a very sensitive heart surgery,* the doctor on the other end had told her when she asked.

Indu was not a fool. She knew that her husband had a drinking problem, but he also cherished his job immensely and took his work very seriously. She simply couldn't believe that he had reached a point where his drinking affected his work to such a severe degree. The doctor who had called their home was an acquaintance of the family and told Indu that she should consider talking to Kartik about rehab. He had tried, but Kartik had stormed out of the hospital at the mention of it. Indu was more dismayed than anything else. It was as though all her previously internalized fears of Kartik being a chronic alcoholic had been made into a reality simply because the alcohol had affected his work. The reality was that he was always an alcoholic, but now he was no longer a functioning one. He had let his personal life spill over into his professional life, and Indu was at a loss for what to do. She knew that Asha shouldn't come home today, so she spoke to Mrs. Singh in hopes that Asha would be allowed to stay with Priya for an extra night.

Asha still remembered how she had refused to listen to her mother's request and had gone home in the afternoon that day only to find her mother sobbing at the kitchen table with a cup of untouched cold tea in front of her. Her father had left the house without explaining anything to Indu, not knowing that the hospital had called while he was asleep. Of course, Indu had told her daughter everything. This wasn't the sort of thing that could remain hidden for long, especially when Kartik Kaur was such a high-profile doctor. It would be in the local news. He would have great difficulty finding another job. But at that point, Asha, even as a teenager, had only been concerned with getting her father enrolled in rehabilitation. Somehow, she had known that if anyone had a shot of convincing her father to make this decision, it was her.

It was impossible for Asha not to reflect on her father's undoing given Jitendra's current situation. Asha was back at her writing desk, her reflection written in full to Deepika, while Jitendra was busy packing in their bedroom.

Dee, the reason I am divulging so much about your grandfather is because I know how hard it is to watch someone you love behave so egregiously, so counter to everything you believe in, and still want to help them in every way possible. That same day I found my mother crying in the kitchen, my father came home sober in the evening and promised her that he would enroll in a rehab program. This was after I had written a brief note to him expressing my concerns and how deeply I cared for him. My father and I had more of a distant relationship than I would have liked in many instances. Notes were the best form of communication for us. He was too curious not to read them, and I was too upset to articulate my arguments verbally without crying and screaming. Despite what he had said to my mother, I lost him before he could uphold his promise.

*I am so sorry that you have to watch **your** father go through this, but there is something we both want you to know. Dad didn't want me to tell you this right away because he values your respect more than you know. He is leaving for rehab tomorrow at Bellwood Health Services. They have estimated that he'll need to be there for at least two months, but that could change and it could be much longer. You can visit him if you feel like it, in fact, he would love to see you. The centre isn't too far from your residence. I know how hard this is, Deepika, but the fact that he has taken this first step is promising.*

Love,
Mom

Asha was satisfied with the letter. This was going to be the first of a few. She intended to write to Deepika until she felt that her daughter was coming back to her. She sealed the envelope and placed it in the drawer. She would mail it out tomorrow. Perhaps all this was old-fashioned considering they all had emails now, but for her to convey such personal details, she needed the entire process to be personal – from her father's pen gliding over the specialty paper from her childhood to her neatly folding the letter away and signing her daughter's name and address in elegant cursive on the front of the envelope. She didn't want to recreate the hollow relationship she had to maintain with her undemonstrative father by sending her daughter a plain email, as if they were colleagues rather than family.

"Hey Ash?" Jeet approached his wife hesitantly as he saw that she was deep in thought. There was vulnerability in his tone that Asha hadn't heard in a while.

Asha looked at him sympathetically, put her writing materials away and got up to give him a hug. She could only imagine his pain right now. He hadn't spoken to Deepika on the phone since dropping her off to university. He was set to leave the two most precious people to him for an uncertain period of time for what was likely to be the biggest fight of his life.

Chapter 5

"Are you going to tell her?" Jeet asked Asha while they were having their last dinner together for a while.

Asha looked up from her meal and gave her husband a small smile that didn't reach her eyes, "We're going to tell her."

Jitendra's eyes could not longer meet Asha's without tearing up. As much as he wanted to tell Deepika about his rehab plans, so that maybe she would forgive him and perhaps even visit him, the thought of him failing and letting his daughter down again was too much. He knew that if he didn't make it through the program, he would be letting his wife down as well, but he needed someone. She was the only one who never left his side; even when he didn't deserve her forgiveness, she was there. Deepika, however, was different. She had a feisty spirit and wouldn't take anyone's nonsense, especially his. Jeet couldn't help but smile as he thought of his daughter. She had no idea how much he admired her because he had never been taught how to convey those sorts of emotions. His parents had never displayed this kind of affection for him or his sisters, and he knew that part of the reason he could be so distant and cold was because that is what he had grown up seeing.

"What are you thinking about?" Asha spoke up after a few minutes of sitting silently, eating. She reached over the table to grasp Jeet's hand warmly as a reassurance that he could tell her whatever it was he was considering, even if he was thinking of backing out.

"I don't think Deepika will ever forgive me if I tell her that I'm doing this and fail," Jeet smiled sadly, squeezing Ash's hand for comfort.

Asha understood his hesitation, but she also knew that Deepika would be proud of him for just trying. Asha's own father had promised he would try and hadn't ever followed through with it, so this was a big improvement. Their daughter was extremely bright – she knew that addiction wasn't something you could quit in a day, and sometimes, it just never goes away. The fact that she wanted to stay away from her parents for a while was her way of coping, Asha knew this.

"She loves you more than you know," Asha smiled and stood up to take their plates to the sink. Before she left him at the table, she rubbed his back encouragingly and added, "The thought of losing

29

you scares her more than it scares you, Jeet. She just wants to see that you care, and trying this, will do just that. I wouldn't be surprised if she's the first to visit you."

A small smile formed on Jeet's lips, and the doubts he had about pursuing the rehab program vanished at the thought that he could win his daughter's affection back. It had never completely dissipated, it had just diminished to a point where he was terrified that their relationship would emulate the one he had with his parents: a superficial call here and there, going through the motions but not really caring at all. Even though the people who really needed to know about the challenge he was about to embark on already knew, he felt some urge to call his parents. At the end of it all, if it was just Ash that was with him, he would be able to survive it. All these thoughts occupied his mind nearly every day after his D.U.I., but he was unable to convey them explicitly to anyone. He could tell that Ash understood, however, and sometimes he was so thankful for that implicit connection they had because it had saved their marriage more than once that the thought of losing her brought an unimaginable amount of dread into his heart that he couldn't shake for days at a time.

"You should call your parents, Jeet," Asha said from the kitchen as soon as she turned the faucet off.

Jitendra's pensive expression quickly turned into a smirk as he replied, "Good idea."

The phone call didn't go well. In fact, it went so poorly that, at one point, Asha took the phone from her husband and tried reasoning with his parents. Dev and Archana were difficult people. They were the sorts of parents that had trouble admitting their children were wrong, and so, the rest of the world had issues according to them. But their children. Their children were always perfect in their eyes. Therefore, the thought of their precious Jitendra packing up, leaving his work, and going off to rehabilitation was absurd. Rehab was for people who had serious self-control deficiencies, actual health problems that interfered with their daily routines. That was what Dev Jha had conveyed to Asha on the phone in a particularly rude manner, as if she were to blame for their son's alcoholism.

Jitendra's experience speaking to his parents was more disillusioning than anything else. They had actually told him that he didn't have a problem. *What nonsense, Jeet! Has Asha put this ridiculous idea into your head? Rehab! That is for alcoholics – people who don't work and sit in their vomit-ridden clothes all day. Who is she to speak? You make the larger income! Who is she without you?* Dev's way of convincing Jitendra that he didn't have a problem was to compare him to the extreme case of a completely dysfunctional alcoholic. The breaking point for him, the point at which he told Asha that he was going to hang up unless she wanted to speak to them, was when his mother, Archana, had the audacity to blame Asha for his arrest. She had argued that Asha must have called the cops. How else could they have found her son in such a remote area?

Jitendra had truly believed that maybe this incident would be the one to spark a change in his parents' incomprehensible disdain for Asha, and on top of that, perhaps it would have made them realize that he wasn't a perfect man. Perhaps it would have been the one thing that would finally make them tell him that he was wrong. He was so tired of hearing how perfect and wonderful he was – didn't they realize that this was why he had turned out so spoilt and stubborn? He would never be able to admit to his daughter that he admired her for telling him he was wrong. As much as he found it difficult to hear, he knew she really cared for and loved him just because, like Ash, she told him his flaws and wanted to help him fix them. Deepika was the first one he saw after the DUI. She was the one who had picked him up from the police station because his wife was too hurt, too utterly heartbroken to come for him herself. And for some reason, Deepika couldn't bear the thought of letting her father suffer in a jail cell for a night despite how angry she was with him. *I blame myself for this.* Jitendra heard the words his daughter had told him when he had gotten into the car again, and he felt immense pain in his chest as he recalled the worst night of his life.

August 10, 2016. This was the day that changed Jitendra's life entirely. He was hosting a large office party for his employees, as the summer was coming to an end. He had invited a bunch of his close friends as well because that's how he was. When there was an opportunity to get everyone together and alcohol was involved, Jitendra would be sending out emails to his favourite people, and of course they would come because which person doesn't love free booze, decent food, and a good time? He either didn't notice or chose to ignore the fact that he never received an invitation of the same grandeur. Then again, none of his friends had the means or desire to blow the same amount of money Jitendra did so often.

The dinner party was at The Keg, the popular steakhouse and bar, in North York. Popular, in that Jitendra enjoyed lunches with clients, among others, there on a weekly basis. He knew most of the staff as well as the manager. Deepika had witnessed this one afternoon when she had gone to work with him over the summer in order to make use of the high-speed Internet because it was down at home. They had walked into the restaurant with one of her father's employees and friends – it was hard to tell the difference at times – and upon approaching the waitress receiving customers at the front, they had been greeted with such warmth and familiarity that Deepika couldn't help but admire her father's ability to connect with so many people. She had told him so. She had said that it was commendable that he could make any stranger laugh, whether ten years old or fifty. It was a great skill to have in business. He had thanked her and joked that perhaps the capability was written in her genes. They had then enjoyed a glass of wine and a juicy cut of steak together, and Jitendra had never really been able to tell his daughter, but he had been delighted at the fact that the Internet hadn't been working at home that day.

The manager was ecstatic of course. About half the restaurant was booked, and the bar area was already full of eager couples. Jitendra had extended the invitation not only to his friends, who had nothing to do with his business, but also to his employees' spouses. Asha had been asked as well, but she and Deepika had made their own plans prior to knowing about it. Plus, they were so used to these summer parties that this particular one was nothing special. For someone who ran a small business, one would think Google's CEO was hosting a dinner for executives given the number of people in the restaurant. Despite it being a waste, Deepika enjoyed attending some of these events. She knew she had to be careful. She was Jitendra's daughter – she was prone to addictive behaviour, it was written in her genes. So she had to control herself, and she did, although some nights she enjoyed getting drunk with her family or her friends. Family bonding, she would consider it, because sometimes she felt that was the only time she could truly connect

32

with her father. When both their inhibitions were nonexistent.

Some time around 1 A.M., only Jitendra and his close buddy from high school were left finishing their last scotch. The manager had made a special exception for Jeet, extending the bar hours to 2 A.M. It was almost closing time, and his friend asked him whether he wanted to share a cab home, but he refused saying that he he'd already called one for himself. It wasn't a lie. For some reason the cab never showed up, and so, an exhausted, but an absolutely plastered Jitendra decided that he'd get home himself. He didn't want to bother his wife this late, and he'd texted Deepika to see if she was awake but she hadn't responded. Inebriated past the point of possibility for any sort of sound judgment, he thanked the manager in a surprisingly coherent manner and got into his car without taking a pause to think of an alternative. He struggled with the keys momentarily, but managed to get the car started. He didn't bother with his seatbelt and proceeded to drive home.

Somewhere between getting into his car and seeing his furious daughter barge into a Toronto police station, Jitendra had been pulled over for reckless driving. He had been speeding and weaving in and out of his lane. A Good Samaritan had called the cops to report the suspicious driving activity because in that remote area, at such a late hour, there were minimal cars on the road and no police officers in sight. The officer had managed to reach Deepika on her cell after Asha had refused to pick her husband up. He conveyed to Jitendra, in the most disciplining and harsh manner possible, that he was lucky that his daughter had such a good kind heart, better than what he deserved, to agree to pick him up at this hour, to even see him at all. Jitendra listened to the cop with a stunned expression, all the while wondering how on earth he would be able to face his daughter. It wasn't long before she showed up at the station, glanced at him indifferently, and walked out with him following her meekly as soon as he was released from the cell.

"0.08 BAC, 3-day roadside suspension, $180 fine," Deepika listed to a silent Jitendra before turning the ignition on, "That's quite lenient, if you ask me."

She was boiling with anger, he could see that. It was almost worse that she wasn't screaming at him. He deserved it. No, what he really deserved was to have been left in jail that night and feel solitary confinement, surrounded by the cold cell walls, with nothing but the sounds of police officers ordering him around like a dog. That would have given him a taste of what his life could be like if he kept driving his family away. They drove in silence for a while. It was almost 7 A.M. at this point. Deepika had only received the call at 4:30 in the morning. Her father had passed out in the jail cell for a good three hours before she had come to get him. Deepika stopped at a Starbucks and bought them each a grande Americano Misto and a sandwich for her father. *Why is she being so nice to me,* Jitendra thought, taking the food and drink from her daughter with the most blank and surprised expression on his face. *Because she's completely given up on you,* another voice entered his head. He was trying to fight back tears. Jitendra Jha didn't cry in front of people, especially his daughter.

"The worst part of all this," Deepika started, looking straight ahead at the road even though Jitendra had turned to look at her for the first time in the car ride, "Is that part of me wishes I had been awake to get your incomprehensible text. I blame myself for this. I knew how weak you were and how the odds of you making this kind of selfish decision weren't that low, and yet, I was out with my friends partying instead of picking you up myself."

Now Jitendra couldn't take it. The tears he had been holding back fell quietly. He was a shitty father. His daughter actually believed, or at least some part of her did, that she should be worrying about how he gets home after these gatherings of his. After a good ten minutes, just as they approached the intersection by their home, Jitendra turned to look at his daughter and managed to mumble a soft apology. He didn't expect her to acknowledge it whatsoever, but what she said afterwards hurt him more than silence would have.

At the red light, she looked gravely into her father's eyes with and said, "I'm sorry too."

Chapter 6

It had only been a few days since Asha and Jitendra had dropped Deepika off to university, but it felt like ages since they had driven together. This time Asha was the one driving that god-awful Range Rover Jeet had bought in the spur of the moment. She did not understand why both Jeet and Dee had such a fondness for the massive, gas-guzzling, obnoxiously loud vehicle. Then again, she had never cared much for cars. As long as it could get her from point A to point B without being a safety hazard, she was fine with it.

Asha glanced over at her husband and almost asked him how he was feeling, but when she saw the thoughtfulness in his eyes and the tranquil way in which he was gazing out the window with his elbow resting on the window's ledge and his open palm supporting the side of his face, she decided against speaking, avoiding the possibility of interrupting his peace, or at least the semblance of it. Jitendra was surprisingly calm considering the fact that he was being driven directly to Hell, and that too, by his wife. Yet he figured that the amount of hell he had given his wife and daughter could not come even remotely close to the little he would have to endure in order to save himself and his family. *Hell is other people*, Deepika had once quoted the famous existentialist, Jean-Paul Sartre in a discussion with her parents during her birthday dinner. That quote had stuck with Jitendra ever since his daughter had mentioned it. Perhaps the relevance of it had propelled the memory of their discussion into Jeet's mind at the most random of moments.

"Hmm, that's quite the statement," Jeet smiled at his daughter as he dug into his pomodoro pasta dish, "It definitely makes a lot of sense."

"Yeah, I know! There's so much to learn from literature, Dad. If you like that quote, I can send you tons of others. I made a list of my favourites, but I'm sure you'll recognize many of them from my Facebook feed!" Deepika responded, excitedly. She almost spilled some of her wine when she reached for her glass.

They were out for Deepika's 19th birthday that evening, and of course, once the topic of her studies came up, pure passion radiated from her. Jitendra felt himself pulled into the conversation. He could never engage her in his favourite political conversations the way she could capture his interest when she spoke of the classics she adored so much. She had a particular affinity for the French writers, being so intrigued by the language, and Asha couldn't help but take some of the credit for having passed on her copy of *The Stranger* to Deepika. Not only did Dee read the English version her mother had given her, but she also purchased the original French text and analyzed it entirely. Indu had never fully appreciated the novel, at least not to the degree Deepika did.

"You know, I also read *The Stranger* before your mother gave you her copy," Jitendra said. He paused to take a sip of his scotch, and then added, "There is not love of life – "

"Without despair of life!" Deepika and her father finished the quote in unison, "He's a genius."

Deepika's eyes were shining, and Asha couldn't wipe the smile off her face when she watched Jeet and Dee bond over Deepika's favourite things on her birthday. The best part was that Jeet wasn't intentionally trying this hard to please his daughter on her special day. He genuinely enjoyed what his daughter was studying, and Deepika could see that he wasn't feigning interest. Jitendra was a well-read man, but he stuck to certain authors and confined himself to very specific genres. Choosing to opt out of post-secondary studies hadn't made him any less smart or determined than his friends, but perhaps it limited his worldview and the exposure to different perspectives. It was only when Dee explained her studies to him and Ash that he, out of sheer curiosity, picked up her reading list one day and made himself a copy. He had made it halfway down the list by her 19th birthday and intended to complete it by the time her course was complete.

Asha turned into the driveway of Bellwood Health Services cautiously, as the area around it was teeming with cars. She hated driving in downtown Toronto. There were too many pedestrians, bikers, and reckless drivers around for her to feel comfortable, especially when she was stuck driving the monster of an SUV her husband and daughter adored so much. She could have dropped Jeet off in her small silver Volvo, but she knew that this was his last chance to sit in his Rover for a while, so she didn't hesitate in her decision. They had both agreed that it would be best if she drove, as his focus would be elsewhere, naturally.

"Ready?" Asha squeezed Jeet's hand, which had curled up into a fist. His grip instinctively loosened upon her touch.

"If not now, when?" Jeet gave Asha a brief smile and then said, "What was it Camus wrote? After a while you could get used to anything? I am so sorry you and Dee got so used to my unforgivable behaviour, and if you could do that, then I can definitely try to get used to…this."

He had trouble acknowledging that he was entering into rehab. This was something he would never have seen himself participating in. He just hoped that all the movies he had seen mocking the process were exaggerations because the thought of sitting in a circle with a bunch of strangers and introducing himself as an alcoholic was so repulsive that he knew he wouldn't make it past the first day if that's how it began. Inside the facility, a much too excited volunteer greeted him and Ash and led them to the registration area. *This isn't a goddamn welcome week residence tour,* Jeet thought, looking pointedly annoyed. Asha could practically read his thoughts and nudged him enough to get him to stop frowning. They approached the reception desk slowly while Jeet took in his surroundings. The place actually resembled Deepika's residence at U of T. Jitendra was not impressed, but he had expected nothing better. Compared to his beautiful house in North York, this place felt more or less like an inn, and that didn't sit well with him. He only hoped that he would be able to stick to the treatment plan so he could get out as soon as possible.

"Hello, Jitendra," a jubilant-looking woman in a lab coat greeted him with a handshake, "I'm Barbara. I'll be your Admissions Counsellor this morning. We just need to do an assessment before we can determine a specific treatment plan for you."

Jitendra forced a smile and tried not to let too much sarcasm seep through his voice before exclaiming, "Sounds great!"

Barbara then looked over at Asha and smiled when Asha introduced herself with another handshake. The counsellor displayed every emotion Jitendra was lacking. The smile on her face hardly ever diminished during their entire conversation, even when Jeet gave her basic yes or no responses to questions that required elaboration. She was a plump woman with blonde hair that must have been touched up regularly, and Jeet guessed that she was the kind of woman to invest in bottles upon bottles of Olay anti-aging cream to no avail. The persistent wrinkles and the bags under her eyes gave her age away. She must have been at least Jitendra's age if not a few years his elder. While Jitendra was more focused on assessing his counsellor and surroundings, Barbara was busy finishing up his treatment plan.

"Well, Mr. Jha, I am delighted to tell you that if you stick to the plan and things are working well, you could be out of here in as little as two months!"

Asha was ecstatic to hear this; she had originally thought that after assessing Jeet's drinking habits, the estimate she had originally been given would have been tossed out the window and instead he'd be told he'd be in there for half a year or something ridiculously long. She caressed her husband's shoulder lovingly and grinned at him before saying, "I know you can do this, Jeet."

Jeet smiled at his wife's encouragement, but two months seemed to be far too long. He was sure his disappointment was written all over his face, and he didn't even bother trying to hide it this time.

"Don't worry, Mr. Jha, your family can come and visit you after the first week. The two months will fly by, and you'll meet some very nice people here. You aren't alone," Barbara's voice had become irritating at this point. This whole situation was becoming too real for Jitendra to process it. He wanted to go to his room. *No, he wanted to go home.*

"I do need to lay down some ground rules before our volunteers show you to your room, Jitendra. Firstly, we don't allow cell phone use in the facility. You are able to use our phones at certain times, unless there is an emergency of course. No visitations until the end of week one. We've found that it makes it easier for our residents to adjust to the program if they don't contact loved ones right away."

The rest of Barbara's rules blurred together. Jitendra had stopped listening after her visitation rules. If there was any consolation left for him, it was that Deepika was an hour away by bus and even less so by car and that he was certain Ash would come to see him. An hour later, Jitendra was left to his thoughts in his tiny dorm-like room with his suitcase unpacked and his clothes put away neatly, thanks to Asha. She had left him with a tight embrace, a quick kiss, and a few words: *Don't do this for me, Jeet. Don't do it for Deepika. Do this for yourself.* What she might never understand is that he couldn't do it for himself. He could only do it for his wife and daughter. His sense of self-worth, his value, and any desire he had to do the right thing came from Asha and Deepika. He knew it was problematic to think that way, but he couldn't pin the blame for the lack of care he had for himself on anyone other than maybe his parents. After all, they had never displayed real love, true affection, towards him the way his wife and daughter did. Alone in his room, without a phone to scroll through to keep him distracted, he rummaged through the desk drawer's in front of him. He found a deck of cards and a pad of paper with a couple of pens. He chuckled softly. This room was better suited for Deepika to write her songs and poetry than it was for him, he thought. The only thing left to do was take a nap, he supposed, so he lay down on the single bed's tough mattress and closed his eyes, but sleep didn't come so easily.

"Anita, hurry up! We have to leave for school!" Jitendra called his 8-year old sister, who was fumbling with her backpack as she rushed into the kitchen, her two pigtails bobbing up and down as she ran to get her shoes.

Jitendra shook his head in frustration as he watched his little sister struggle with her shoelaces. The 12-year old boy hated being late to anything and school was no exception. He dropped his things with a heavy sigh and helped his sister with her shoes.

"Is Gaurav Uncle taking care of us today?" Anita asked, innocently. It was the second day for Jitendra and Anita without their parents in India. Dev and Archana had gone abroad to Canada to seek sponsorship from Archana's sister who had immigrated there a few years prior. Dev Jha had explained to his son that it was necessary that he take good care of his sister while they were gone, him being the eldest child. However, his father had never mentioned anything about taking care of himself or the fact that he was just that – a child. Thankfully for Jitendra, his parents had taken his two-year old sister, Gauri, with them. It was enough to manage Anita on his own. They would only be gone a week, Dev had told his son. On top of that, they had requested for their friends in the closely-knit Chandigarh neighbourhood to check in on their children. Jitendra's favourites, Gaurav Uncle and Sunita Aunty, had even offered to take care of their dinners. Last night, they had come over in the evening, and Sunita had cooked a large pot of butter chicken and rice and had ordered fresh naans from a nearby restaurant. Jitendra made sure to keep the leftovers in the fridge afterwards, so that he and Anita would have lunch for the next two days.

"Gaurav Uncle and Sunita Aunty are having us over tonight for dinner, Anita. But remember this, I will always be here to take care of you. We take care of each other," Jitendra spoke, as he zipped up his sister's jacket. His sister smiled at him, and they both walked hand-in-hand to school singing their favourite Punjabi songs.

Jitendra opened his eyes and stared at the ceiling. Delving this deep into his subconscious was not something he was prepared to do in this strange place, surrounded by dreary white walls and the sound of his past traumas colliding with one another, reminding him why he was stuck where he was. Jeet didn't realize he was sweating until he ran his fingers through his hair and felt an unprecedented amount of moisture coat his fingertips. He let out a dissatisfied groan and lamented to himself. How in the world was he supposed to sleep on this uncomfortably tough mattress when he was used to the feeling of memory foam and Ash next to him, to chat with when they both couldn't sleep? If Hell was other people, then let him be thrown into the fiery pits and burn. He would rather have that than solitary confinement.

He stood up and looked through his suitcase to see if he brought anything that would distract him from his unpleasant childhood memories; to his surprise, he found a piece of paper sticking out of the lining of the suitcase. He pulled it out curiously and found that it was addressed to him from Asha: *Jeet, look in the lining of the suitcase. I wasn't sure if it was allowed, but I know it will help you tremendously. Love, Ash.* What could she have meant? Jeet felt around in the lining of the suitcase and finally felt a pair of earphones and something else. He retrieved his mini white iPod shuffle attached to a pair of earphones as well as a small portable charger that he could plug into the wall discreetly. His entire mood shifted the second he saw his iPod. He couldn't believe that Ash had thought of something like that, but at the same time, he wasn't that surprised that she had. She knew him best, after all. He was beyond thrilled and even more so excited to see what Ash had downloaded for him. He plopped onto the bed, which didn't feel as uncomfortable or small now. He hit play and couldn't control the big smile forming on his lips when he heard his favourite Led Zeppelin. He was suddenly transported into this gorgeous car, drumming his fingers against the steering wheel with the windows rolled all the way down so that he could inhale the sweet scent of summer. Adjusting his sunglasses, he glanced at himself in the rear view mirror and grinned before belting out the chorus of "Babe I'm Gonna Leave You," one of his favourite tracks.

While Jitendra was adapting to his temporary home, Asha was nearing home. She had stopped at a post office a couple of days ago to mail the letter she had written for Deepika. She recalled how she had written the address on the envelope neatly, placed the required stamps carefully in the appropriate corner, and sealed the envelope with a sticker. Hesitating for only a second or two, she had let the letter fall into the mailbox. She smiled as she drove, thinking about Deepika reading it shortly. Everything would get better from today on.

Chapter 7

The house felt strange when Asha entered it, as though she had inadvertently swapped keys with a stranger and entered a foreign space that she didn't particularly like. It seemed darker, even after she had turned all the lights on; colder, even after retrieving a shawl and sitting by the fireplace with a cup of steaming hot chai; and quieter, uncomfortably so, despite Eva Cassidy's "Autumn Leaves" pouring through the vacant house. First, it had been Deepika who had left for school. Eventually, both Jitendra and Asha had adjusted to the significant increase in silence and the lack of liveliness at home. They had had a lot of trouble in the beginning. Deepika had never minded quiet time. In fact, she enjoyed reflecting and daydreaming, but when the family was in a room together, or when she just wanted to sing along to her favourite artists while they put on a private concert for her parents through the in-home stereo system, her voice would raise everyone's spirits, especially Asha's.

Asha could never fully get used to Jitendra's lack of conversation when he wasn't drinking, so when Deepika made the effort to speak about anything, she would engage her happily. Asha laughed to herself when she thought of the numerous times both she and her daughter scolded Jitendra for being so serious about some football game or the other that he would silently stare at the screen, frowning, as though he were the coach and his team was losing. Now, sitting alone in the family room, Asha couldn't help but miss Deepika's energy, her adoration for music, and her fun-loving jabs at her parents, as well as herself, when they told her that unfortunately, she did not have Adele's voice, and so, she'd better concentrate on her studies. It was all in good spirit, though. Dee would laugh it off, return to her room, and pick up her guitar and sing along for hours. Sometimes, Asha would be upstairs doing some household chores and stop to listen for a few minutes. Her daughter's singing voice wasn't terrible when she actually tried her best, but what surprised Asha the most, were the lyrics she would sing. Although Asha didn't know every single artist Dee listened to, the lyrics resonated so much that they must have been original. They were poetic, they were raw, and the passion behind them couldn't have been emulated. That night she had asked Dee about the song she'd been singing, saying

43

that it was very nice, and she had been met with a blush and a modest, *I wrote it.* Asha had learned that her daughter not only wrote poetry, as she did, but also songs, stories, A-grade papers; she couldn't have been more proud.

Her thoughts shifted to Jitendra the second she heard the acoustic beginnings of "Stairway to Heaven". She was sure that sending his iPod with him would make his stay somewhat bearable, if not significantly better. Three months ago, before the DUI, she couldn't imagine him doing so much as looking at a rehab website, and now he was spending his first night at the Toronto centre. Even if he didn't finish it, even if he called her one day in the middle of the treatment plan and told her it was torture and that he couldn't bear it, she would be proud of him for trying because that was something her father had been too far gone to attempt.

December 23, 1987. Two days before Christmas. The Kaur family loved celebrating the holidays. Christmas was like a second Diwali. Any chance the Kaur family had to bring their relatives together, they would take it. Their small tree was up, thanks to Asha and Indu. Kartik would admire their efforts – it was hard not to be mesmerized every time he entered the foyer of their apartment's suite when the tree was lit up with hues of deep purple and blues. The holidays meant eating, drinking, and laughing with family. Christmas was supposed to be a happy occasion, and it had always been so, until this year. Asha was in the kitchenette, helping Indu prepare a traditional Christmas dinner – turkey and all – despite being happy with eating Indian food every day of the week, Kartik enjoyed the occasional change. Indu wasn't much of a meat-eater, so she made a vegetable mix and potatoes as well. Kartik was out with some friends that evening but had promised that he'd be home in time for dinner. When he had mentioned that he'd be out in the evening, Indu had not been happy. She'd scolded him and commented that his friends seemed to be a hell of a lot more important than his family, and why on earth were these idiotic friends of his going out with him two days before Christmas when they should also be with their families. He had simply responded that he didn't have the energy to fight and that he was off. Within minutes, Indu had been left standing in the living room with her eyebrows knitted together and deep frown lines in her forehead that became more prominent when

Kartik slammed the door more loudly than usual. Of course, as she got cooking with Asha, her anger at Kartik faded and she was looking forward to their family dinner.

In the middle of their cooking, just as Asha was about to put some of her favourite 80s music on, mother and daughter jumped simultaneously when they heard three loud bangs on the door. Asha glanced at her watch and frowned. It was too early for Papa to be home, let alone for their neighbours to arrive. Indu asked her to get the door, so she bounded over with a huge smile on her face, ready to greet the friend or stranger behind the door. As soon as it was revealed who was behind the door, Asha's smile quickly turned into a look of pure concern, and anxiety washed over her. Two officers, who looked equally troubled, as well as one of Kartik's colleagues from the hospital, whose eyes were crimson red and whose cheeks glistened with fresh tears, stood outside and wordlessly asked to be invited in.

"Who is it?" Indu called from the kitchen, completely unawares.

When she received no response, she bustled into the sitting area with the same enthusiasm Asha had displayed before seeing who their guests were. As soon as Indu saw Kartik's colleague and good friend, Rahul, and the obvious fact that he had been crying, she knew something was terribly wrong and tears escaped her eyes before so much as finding out what had happened. It couldn't have been good if the police were there. They all sat down; still, nothing had been said. Asha was experiencing shock. She could not cry nor move from her seat. Her 19 year-old mind was imaging all sorts of things, but the one she most feared could not have been true. And yet, it was.

Kartik Kaur had not gone to see his friends that evening. Instead, he had gone to a local pub around 6 P.M. to drink away his sorrows after losing his job at the hospital and finding that it was nearly impossible to find work at other hospitals or even smaller medical clinics, at least not the kind of fulfilling work he wanted to do, after being fired. The officers had found him after a few locals had called the station to report a car crash by the underpass near the DLF flats complex. They had run to the car to see if the driver was okay, but the flames devouring the front of the car and the clouds of thick smoke surrounding it had made it too hard to see the driver's condition. The underpass wasn't usually busy, so the officers had ruled out any kind of traffic-related accident. It was a dark area with hardly any natural light at that time of night. There were solitary lampposts, whose bulbs needed changing, on either side of the underpass, just before entering the dark tunnel, and tiny lights lining the sides of it to guide drivers through to the other side. Kartik hadn't even made it into the underpass; he had lost control of his car right outside and had crashed into a nearby tree. When the ambulance had arrived and the paramedics managed to retrieve his body, anyone could see that there wasn't any chance of him surviving. The speed at which he had been travelling and the impact with which he had collided into the tree would have made it a miracle if he had been breathing when the emergency response team had found him. The smoke had already penetrated his lungs to nearly full capacity. The police report that was filed at the time of the incident cited inebriation as the main reason for the accident after alcohol was found in Kartik's system.

Asha and Indu were beyond distraught as they waited for Rahul to bring more news at the hospital. Kartik hadn't officially been declared deceased, and Indu was praying for some sort of divine intervention to save her husband. Asha already knew it was over. Her father was dead. She had lost her dad at 19 years old, just a teenager, barely ready for the real world. She had hardly had enough time to learn from him, but he had taught her the toughest lessons of all: how to cope with loss and how to grieve.

When Rahul came out of the hospital room with wet streaks running down his face and nothing but a slight shake of the head and a low murmur of an apology, Asha finally allowed herself to cry with her mother. Rahul came over and hugged the young girl tightly, without a word. He wasn't about to tell her that it would be okay, or that she would heal in time. None of that clichéd nonsense, not when he was sure she'd hear it from her neighbours and friends a million times over after the shock of it all had passed. After a few minutes, he simply said, "He loved you, Ash."

Any doubt that Asha had about Kartik not caring enough about her or her interests vanished when Rahul said that. Rahul and Kartik spent so much time together both at the hospital and outside of work that Asha knew that he wasn't just spouting words of comfort to make her feel better. A few hours later, Indu and Asha's closest friends had come to the hospital to offer their support and say goodbye to Kartik. Rahul returned after a bit to ask Asha if she wanted to say bye to her father alone, to see him one last time. At first, she was uncertain whether she was prepared to see his lifeless body lying on a cold hospital table, but she knew that she had to do this, otherwise she would regret it forever.

They walked into the morgue together. Rahul squeezed Asha's shoulder reassuringly and gave her some time alone after confirming if she was okay to be there alone. She nodded and stepped closer to Kartik's body. She had never seen death so up close in her life. She had read descriptions of it, seen countless movies depicting it, had even talked about it with her friends. But to see a loved one, unmoving, cold to the touch, frozen, that was a dreadful experience. His body was lying there in front of her, and yet, the experience felt nightmarish and unreal. She couldn't absorb it. She reached out to touch his hand and jumped slightly at the temperature. He was warmer than she expected. She had expected to feel ice. Then again, he had only died hours ago. Papa was dead. She repeated it in her head many times, but it wouldn't sink in. She pictured her life without her father, a day from now, a month, a year. He would never walk through their apartment door with his medical coat on. He would never throw his stethoscope carelessly onto the couch and prop himself in front of the TV. He would never ask for his favourite whiskey on ice, or ask her to sit and chat with him, or scold her for not doing as well as he knew she was capable of on her science tests again. She grasped her father's bloodless hand and sobbed. What was the last thing she had said to him? That she hoped he would complete the rehab for his own sake. He had smiled at her and said, *Yes, beta, for my sake, and for yours, and for your mother's. I will.*

"Ash, are you alright?" Rahul's voice interrupted her memory and prompted her to wipe her tears and let go of her father's hand.

"I want to go," she replied, heading towards the exit, unable to stop the tears from flowing no matter how hard she tried to wipe them away. They were endless, and she didn't have the energy to keep dabbing tissues at them.

"Of course," Rahul spoke softly and led her out of the room into the lobby, "Ash, your Papa had something for you. A gift. We retrieved some bags from the trunk of his car. Would you like to see it?"

Asha couldn't care less about Christmas gifts at the moment, but the thought of holding onto something tangible, something her father had hand-picked for her himself, that made her agree to Rahul's question. Rahul then presented her with a little note and a rectangular black box with silver text on the outside. She opened the note first.

Dear Ash,
Promise me you'll never stop writing. Study hard, but never stop writing. Write from your heart, everyday. You have too much to offer for you not to share it with the world. Write to your heart's content.
Love,
Papa.

Rahul then handed her the box. She read the silver inscription on the top and smiled while allowing the tears to fall. Parker 75. The beautiful fountain pen she had been asking for since the summer. He had shushed her when she was talking about it at first because he wasn't happy about some of her marks, but he had remembered the name, the colour, and the exact model she had mentioned. All this time Asha had thought that her father hadn't heard her, hadn't truly understood her, but he had. He had listened at times when she thought no one was. He had loved her more than she'd known.

Asha rubbed her eyes, realizing that she had fallen into a reverie that she hadn't had in a while. She'd been ignoring the memory, pushing it into the depths of her subconscious because it was so painful. She'd pushed it so far away that she'd forgotten the good parts, the happy moments. She sat up in her seat by the fireplace and got up to make another cup of tea. Just as she left the family room, the doorbell rang. She glanced at her watch, wondering who it could be this evening. She hadn't called anyone over. She shrugged and walked over to the door, not bothering to peer through the peephole as she usually did.

"Hi, Mom," Deepika stood outside smiling, with a small suitcase in one hand and the letter Asha had sent her in the other.

Chapter 8

"Dee?" Asha couldn't believe her eyes when she saw her daughter standing in front of her. It had only been a week since she'd gone back to university. Usually Asha would expect a month to go by before seeing Deepika at their house, sometimes almost two. They would of course meet her for lunches downtown in the meantime. It wasn't that Deepika didn't want to see her parents or talk to them; it was that she didn't want to live in their home because all she was used to seeing was something broken. She'd tried to put the pieces back together so many times but the glue wouldn't stick.

Deepika just smiled at her spellbound mother again and responded playfully, "Are you going to let me in? It's chilly out here."

Asha laughed at her daughter's statement and snapped out of her temporary paralysis. She stepped aside and watched Deepika bustle into the house with her luggage. When she saw that her daughter's hands were free, she held her arms out for a hug and couldn't hold back the silent streaks of saline from dripping down her cheeks. She wiped them away so fast that Deepika hadn't seen. She didn't want to seem like she was upset because she was anything but that.

"Gosh, why on earth is it so dark in here?" Deepika glanced around the living room, hurried to the kitchen to light some candles, and turned on a few lamps on the way, "And what is this depressing music?" She stopped the CD player, plugged her iPhone into the stereo system instead, and put on her collection of jazz covers by Diana Krall.

Asha couldn't stop beaming at the fact that Deepika was home. She chuckled as she watched her daughter light up the entire room. Deepika flitted from one side of the living room to the other, lighting a candle here and there, adjusting the music, and bringing blankets over to the couch for the two of them. Meanwhile, Asha went into the kitchen to finish making the tea that she had intended to before the arrival of a lovely surprise, who was now relaxing by the fire. When Asha returned to the family room, Deepika stood up and hugged her mother once more and thanked her for the tea. They were both quiet for a while, Deepika watching the fire crackle and hiss, engrossed in the fluctuating intensity of the flames, while

50

Asha's gaze alternated between the flames and the letter that Deepika had placed on the side table by the couch. A few minutes later, Asha couldn't bear the silence any longer. She'd been sitting in solitude the entire day after saying goodbye to Jitendra. The music she'd had on repeat only provided so much comfort. After all, it was so much nicer to listen to in the company of loved ones. It had more meaning, more feeling to it when one was in the arms of a lover, or conversing with a child. Deepika's eyes still reflected the fire when Asha glanced at her again before opening her mouth.

"How long are you staying?" Asha asked, leaning back slightly in her rocking chair.

Deepika's attention shifted to her mother as soon as the first word left her mother's mouth. She had been debating whether to start the conversation and how to do it. There was so much she wanted to know, particularly about her grandfather, whose name was hardly ever spoken.

"For the weekend, I have to be back on Monday," Deepika paused for a second. She hesitated to ask what she wanted to. Asha was happy to hear that Deepika would be home for a couple of days. That meant that she wouldn't have to think too much about Jitendra because the thought of him alone at the centre, without her support, scared her.

Deepika interrupted her mother's thoughts when she finally gathered the courage to ask, "How's Dad?"

Asha took a breath before answering because she didn't want to have a breakdown in front of her daughter, and then said, "I think he's going to get through this. It's obviously not going to be easy for him. They confirmed their two-month estimation, but they don't allow visitors until the end of the first week."

Deepika nodded, already making a mental note of when she would be able to see her father. She thought it would help him more if she were supportive rather than angry. One of her teachers had once told her that if someone who has done something bad once and never hears the end of it, that is, if people always view this person by their poor choices, the person is less likely to change or improve himself. To give someone hope and support despite their actions, that was the way to maximize the chances of that person bettering himself. It was great advice, she knew that, but it was also hard to follow through with that When a person has hurt you so often, forgiveness gets more difficult and more meaningless each time, to a point where it translates into complacency, and then what hope is there for change? Deepika thought of both perspectives and decided that in this case, it would be best to be there for her father. He was trying.

"So, I read your letter, Mom," Deepika finally said. Asha had been waiting for this to come up.

"Yes, I just needed you to know...everything," Asha forced a small smile to prevent her from showing that she was getting choked up at the memory of her father.

"Thank you for opening up to me, it makes me understand things a bit better. What exactly happened to my grandfather? You never talk about him. Talk to me about him. Sometimes it just helps to get it out," Deepika said, reassuringly. Her expression was sympathetic. She adjusted her position on the couch so that she was sitting closer to her mother. Asha leaned forward and squeezed her daughter's hand before speaking. Because she had recalled the memory so recently, what she focused on was its ending – the Parker 75, her father's love for her, his encouragement to continue doing what she loved. She relayed some of the unpleasant details to Deepika: how Christmas dinner hadn't even begun before she'd found out that her father had died in a tragic accident, how she had known that alcohol had been at the root of it before the cops had said a word, and how her mother had always given Kartik the benefit of the doubt, thinking he was significantly stronger than he truly was. Asha admitted to Deepika that she had had less faith in her father because she was able to look at the situation more objectively than her mother. Indu had loved Kartik to a point where his imperfections, even the major ones, were simply bumps in the road. Indu had believed that they both would survive the ride even after he'd been fired from work, but she'd been the only one to make it.

"Wow," Deepika muttered under her breath. She was speechless. Never in her wildest dreams could she imagine being in her mother's place. How her mother had managed to keep this from her for so long dumfounded her. She didn't know what else to say, so she just added, "I had no idea you went through something so dreadful."

Asha gave her daughter a small smile and said, "How could you have known? I never told you. But I'm glad I did today."

"Are you okay?" Deepika asked, looking at her mom concernedly, "You know, with Dad…"

Asha sighed, "Well it's going to be hard, for both of us, but the fact that he's taken the first step is promising. My father didn't even manage to get there." She stared at the ground for a couple of minutes before she added, "You're old enough now, and that's why I'm having this discussion with you. Sometimes I think back and wonder if your grandfather's death was actually accidental."

Deepika's head shot up to look at her mother. Her eyes had been focused on the fire while her mother narrated her past, and a combination of the heat from the flames and the sentimentality of a past reality she had no knowledge of, had filled them with warm water. When Asha suggested what Deepika thought she had – this possibility that Kartik had intentionally driven into the tree by the underpass – Deepika was shaken. It reminded her of the times her own father would joke about suicide while he was drinking. He'd say something foolish, like if he were ever lost in abyss of unhappiness, he wouldn't tell his family and just off himself. He talked about it like it was nothing, but hearing him say that he wouldn't tell his family how he was feeling felt like the biggest betrayal to Deepika, and it would anger her any time he brought up that nonsense talk that he eventually noticed and stopped bringing it up when she was sitting with him.

"That underpass…it just doesn't make sense," Asha continued after a lull in the conversation. Now that she was actually talking about this, she was revisiting some of her darkest thoughts.

"What was so special about that underpass?" Deepika asked, having never seen where her parents used to live. She'd been to New Delhi just a couple of times, but that was to see her grandmother. She didn't particularly like or appreciate India to the degree her parents did. There was so much of her mother's history that she was unaware of.

"It's just that we used to pass it so often. Your grandfather loved long drives, as well. He'd take the car out and drive for an hour just to get some air, some time to think after a stressful day at the hospital. He would take me for rides sometimes, and he really liked that area around the underpass because it was rarely busy," Asha stopped and laughed, "One time we were driving by it, and Papa was so happy with his new car that he accelerated so fast that a nearby cop heard the revved up engine and gave him a ticket for speeding. After getting the ticket, he swore he'd buy a car with a softer engine."

Deepika smiled at the anecdote. She'd never had the chance to meet her grandfather, but she could see some similarities between them.

"I just think that he went to that area for a reason."

They sat there for a while, quiet again. There was nothing left to say on the topic. It was a lot to absorb for Deepika, but she was glad that her mother could talk to her about it. For the past twenty years, her mother had been there to listen to her and she still was, but it was nice to be able to reciprocate when it came to something this important.

"Okay, enough of that sad talk. What's new with you?" Asha's pensive demeanour switched to one of cheerfulness within minutes. She didn't want to spend the little time she had with her daughter lamenting the past, an unchangeable part of her life, but one that had been essential to her character. She wanted to celebrate the present and the future to come – with her daughter doing so well, it could only be bright.

Asha and Deepika spent the next few hours poking fun at each other and comparing their experiences at university. Deepika had ordered a large pizza and the two of them pigged out without a care and sipped on sparkling white wine while revelling in each other's company. It was nearing midnight and the conversation came to a point where Asha could sit back, do minimal talking, and watch her daughter gush over a boy she had met on the first day of classes. She couldn't help but grin at Deepika's excitement. The wine and the nature of the conversation had made her giddy. It reminded Asha of the way she had felt about her first boyfriend, although remembering the way that had ended, turned her expression grave and her thoughts anxious.

"What's wrong?" Deepika noticed the change right away.

"Oh, it's nothing. I just hope he treats you well. Just be careful, Deepika," Asha pushed her negativity to the side for a while. This wasn't the time to share her heartbreak with Dee.

"Yeah, of course Mom!" Deepika chided her mother playfully for her concern, "I'll be careful, I promise. He's just very sweet. We're only becoming friends, don't get too ahead of yourself."

Asha burst into laughter at her daughter's last comment and teased, "The way you're commending him after just a week, I don't think I'm the one who's getting too ahead of myself!"

Deepika had a great sense of humour and didn't take offense to the statement. They both laughed together at her folly over this boy she'd come to like. His name was William Moreau. He was French-Canadian and had recently moved to Toronto from Quebec City. He was 22 years old, just a year older than Deepika, and had joined the University of Toronto to take some more English courses because he found the language intriguing. He loved English films as well. He'd already completed a computer science degree in Quebec, so he was a part-time student at University of Toronto while he worked, but Deepika had met him at an English studies wine and cheese event.

"He was so charming, Mom. But in a very sweet way, not in a way that felt like he was just trying to woo me. I have a good feeling about him," Deepika continued, finishing the remainder of the wine in her glass.

Asha smiled and was happy for her daughter. She then joked, "I'm happy that you've met a nice guy, Dee. I just hope you aren't so charmed by him because he speaks your second-favourite language!"

Deepika giggled and then said, "Well, it is a plus. But I can help him with English, and he's already helping me with French. We converse in French half the time. C'est vraiment formidable!"

Asha was delighted to see her daughter so happy after just a week of her final year of study. She then asked, "Do you know if he's also involved in the French exchange program you are going on soon?"

Deepika's eyes lit up at the question, and she replied, "I did ask him that! He didn't officially apply, but he said he was thinking of going unofficially for a couple of weeks around that time to visit some of his relatives in Nice."

"That's wonderful. Perhaps your father and I will get to meet him one day!"

Deepika laughed as her imagination ran wild and simply said, "Peut-être."

Asha had learned a few French terms from Deepika and knew enough to understand that her daughter had said *maybe*, and she knew her daughter well enough to know that she was likely dreaming up all sorts of scenarios with this boy. She didn't want her daughter to get hurt, so she reminded her to focus on the friendship and not get carried away, to which Deepika joked, *Yes, yes we've established that I'm the Marianne Dashwood of North York.* Asha chuckled at the Austen reference. They had both read her entire collection of novels in school.

"It's late," Deepika yawned, standing up to put their wine glasses away and throw out the pizza box.

Asha glanced at the clock and saw that it was almost 2 A.M. *Time flies when you're in good company*, she thought. Having Deepika at home had distracted her from thinking too much about Jeet. That was probably a good thing. She stood up and gave Deepika another hug before they called it a night and went upstairs to sleep. Asha wanted this weekend to last longer than just two days, but she knew it would pass in a matter of minutes.

Chapter 9

The weekend had flown by, naturally. Deepika's presence back home in North York was a rare occurrence during the school year, but this time, she had wanted to stay on longer. She'd even proposed calling her friend Juanita and asking her for notes for a couple of days. While Asha had been tempted to give in to her daughter's pleading to stay home for a few more days, she knew that her approval would have been coming from a selfish place, not a motherly one. So Asha pushed Deepika reluctantly out the door, telling her that she needed to study hard now more than ever before winking at her daughter and adding, *don't make that poor William miss you!* Deepika laughed and rolled her eyes while saying, *oh please, he can text me.* After a few more seconds of playful banter, Deepika surrendered and drove away in her favourite car. Asha's smile didn't fade as she waved to her daughter, waiting for the car to disappear from view before retreating into the house.

The house had changed overnight, Asha felt. It was brighter, warmer, and felt like a home. The music hadn't stopped. Asha strained her ear to catch the beginnings of a song that she soon recognized to be Bonnie Tyler's "It's a Heartache". She recalled the way in which Deepika would belt out the 80s tune in the shower last summer after coming to the painful realization that one of her close male friends did not reciprocate her romantic feelings. The passion in Deepika's voice had been so true to real heartbreak that Asha worried about how her daughter would react when a man actually did break her heart. How would her daughter react when a man left her waiting for him with a heart full of love while he couldn't be bothered? She couldn't help but be cynical, even about this French Canadian boy Deepika was praising. She had praised a boy once, had placed him on a pedestal, only to watch him rise and her fall. Thinking about it now, remembering her mother's painful recollection of the events surrounding her own teenage heartbreak, Asha knew that she needed to simply be there for her daughter just as Indu had been there for her.

"Careful, careful!" Indu shouted at the paramedics as they lifted her daughter into the stretcher and quickly pushed her into the ambulance. Indu watched with tears streaming down her face and her hand covering her mouth, "Oh my god, Kartik. Tell me she's going to be okay!"

"Indu, relax. She's just fainted. It's very hard to overdose on antihistamines. I promise you she'll be fine. The hospital is simply a precaution, okay?" Kartik rubbed her wife's shoulders affectionately, reassuring her that their daughter was going to be okay.

The agonizing part of this event was the fact that Asha had done such a thing. How could she even think of taking pills to numb the pain of a break-up? Indu knew what this was about. Priya had called her frantically while she was at work to tell her that Asha was in bad shape and had left school in tears without a word. Of course, then Indu had put two and two together and got more details from Priya. Vivek Singh had dumped her daughter in the worst way possible. He had first cheated on her, and then when Priya had confronted him about that, he'd said that Asha should have known that they were by no means exclusive and never would be because he could never commit to a girl like her. Priya had then slapped the monstrous jerk across the face and had told him that he deserved to be alone for the rest of his life to which the asshole had laughed, along with his equally horrible friends. Indu's fists curled up in a rage when she recalled what had happened to her daughter. How a boy could be so cruel to someone so gentle and loving was beyond her. Kartik's gesture for her to get into the ambulance reminded her where she was and she hurried into the ambulance.

The paramedics were Kartik's friends, so he sat in the front with them while Indu held Asha's hand in the back. She was just 17 years old. Indu believed Kartik when he said that their daughter would be fine, but she'd always taught Asha to never let anyone get to you – that you have value and if a person does not recognize that and uses you, like this monster had, then you let them go because they don't deserve your love, energy, or time. Given the number of times Indu had told Asha that and Asha had agreed, the fact that Indu was now heading to the emergency room with her unconscious daughter all because of a poor reaction to a useless boy was hard to imagine. Indu could not conceive how could Asha have done such a thing. Then again, Indu had never dated. She'd married relatively young. She'd never had a chance to experience real heartbreak the way Asha had. How could she fully understand what it felt like?

"Papa brought you some tea," Indu handed her teary-eyed, red-faced daughter a steaming cup of chai as she sat up in the hospital bed. It had been two hours since they had rushed her to the emergency room. Everything was completely fine. Asha hadn't taken nearly enough of the allergy medication to cause permanent damage. After Indu had cried for several minutes upon Asha's waking, a bout of intense anger washed over her. She cursed Vivek Singh, she scolded her daughter for not thinking more of herself, she criticized herself for not seeing what a manipulative character the boy had been so that she could have put an end to whatever relationship he had had with her daughter. But the anger was temporary. It lasted only minutes, after which, Indu calmed down and talked to Asha about what had happened. She told her how worried she had been, how she'd been screaming at the paramedics and her husband, and how she'd sworn that she'd kill the bastard who drove her daughter to contemplate suicide. When Indu was recounting these events, Asha could hear the screaming and the sirens in her head. It was as if part of her had been conscious while the events her mother was describing had been unfolding.

"Just promise me, Ash, promise me you know in your heart that you deserve so much more," Indu's pleading tone and watery eyes induced the fall of fresh tears in both mother and daughter.

"Of course I know, Mummy. I don't know what came over me. I feel like such a fool for loving him in the first place," Asha sobbed just as Indu tossed the hospital blanket aside so that she could wrap her arms protectively around her daughter, "He really hurt me. He made me feel like I was the only one that mattered to him and then he slept with my classmate."

Indu's rage reignited when she heard how upset her daughter was. Cheating and lying were two of the most heinous crimes one could commit. Vivek Singh had done both, and not just to anyone, but to her precious daughter. Indu took a few minutes to collect herself before speaking because she had screamed enough about this worthless boy.

"Ash, listen to me. He's not worth a single thought in your intelligent and beautiful head. He's not worth a single tear. Here's what you're going to do. You're going to go back to school tomorrow, you're going to ace your classes, you're going to have a lot of fun with your best friend Priya, and you're going to finish your senior year with flying colours, okay?" Indu smiled when Asha's eyes began to light up, and then said, "You have so much potential. You're the kind of person that succeeds in life, not the likes of low-lives like Vivek. He can have all the fun he wants in high school, but no woman is going to take that shit for good. Promise me, you won't take it from him or anyone else."

Asha wiped the remaining tears away and smiled, "I promise."

Indu squeezed her daughter's hand and reminded her that she was always there for her, no matter how bad it got. Just then, Kartik popped his head into the hospital room.

"Rahul and I have just ordered a couple of pistols. This boy is done," Kartik winked at his daughter. When he heard her laugh, he smiled and strode over to the hospital bed to hug his daughter to his chest and whisper, "Don't ever do that to us again, alright? Boys are idiots, Ash. Believe me, I know."

"He's so right," Indu added before rubbing his shoulder affectionately, earning an eye-roll and a smile from her husband.

Asha laughed with her parents and cried into her father's shirt. He was a good man, and sometimes, she wished he'd realize that too, "I love you, Papa."

"We love you too, beta."

Asha felt a small smile creep onto her lips as she remembered how loved she felt in that hospital room. Not that she necessarily needed to come close to death to feel loved. That was a mistake. Yet she knew that something must have been lacking in her to drive her to do such a thing to herself. She'd fallen into an abyss of twisted ideals, thinking that romantic love was the only kind that could make her feel like she belonged somewhere. But she had grown up and realized that if one had to try so hard to impress someone, to prove oneself to someone, that person wasn't the right one. The right person would be able to see what was there without it being thrown in his face. Now, she could worry about Deepika and pray that her new friend didn't break her heart, or she could have faith that her daughter had more self-worth than she had had at that age. She could just remind her daughter that she was there for her because she knew very well, that at the end of the day, one's heart was hard to control. As if taken over by some inexplicable force,

61

Asha found herself propelled to her writing desk with so much to say. Perhaps it was silly to sit and write old-fashioned letters when she could type out an email in a matter of minutes and likely receive a response within a day. Or maybe, it wasn't so hard to believe that Asha could enjoy the anticipation. Mailing out those letters took her mind off Jitendra and gave her something special to look forward to each day after work. Ninety percent of the time, the mailbox was full of useless advertisements and dreaded bills, but the thought of receiving one of Deepika's brightly-coloured envelopes was so exciting that Asha couldn't bother with email.

Dear Dee,

It was so nice to see you over the weekend. I was delighted to hear about the French exchange program, and of course, Mr. Moreau! I am glad you are enjoying yourself. When you told me about William, I couldn't help but think of one of my ex-boyfriends. He knew just what to say to please me, but I was naïve and fell for sweet nothings. William doesn't sound like that kind of guy, but promise me that you will be careful. The charming type is not always the most genuine. When I look back on my own experience, there were warning signs that I ignored because I just liked the feeling of being wanted. That's an easy trap to fall into. I had such good friends and family around me, but that didn't seem to matter. Deepika, I know you always tell me that you would never fall that way. I also thought it could never happen to me, but sometimes people consume us to a degree we cannot understand. I know you two are just friends right now, but as cool as you tried to be, Dee, I know you're head over heels for this guy. Just promise me, you know that you deserve the best. If this boy so much as comes close to hurting you, you know Dad – he'll break out of that rehab centre and hunt him down! Keep me updated on everything, Dee. It's always the highlight of my day!

Love,
Mom

The great thing about writing letters as opposed to using the computer was that Asha was certain that she wouldn't ramble for pages and bore Deepika with her advice. Asha chuckled to herself as she remembered the number of times her English teachers would scold her for her wordiness. *Be concise*, they'd comment. Had she been? Well, she had said what she wanted to say. Reading it over before sealing the envelope, Asha ensured that it didn't sound like she was preaching. That would be the last thing she intended. She slipped the letter into her purse for mailing the next day. It was too late to do so now. As Asha powered everything off in the house and headed to bed, Deepika and her best friend were just about to leave their house for drinks.

"Ready for the Bacardi!!" Juanita shouted as she hurried to the front door where Deepika was half in hysterics and half trying and failing to pull her leather boots on.

"Oh my god, Cruz, I know you think I only drink rum and coke, but I have a very advanced palate," Deepika joked, finally able get her boots on.

"Oh, right. I totally forgot. You also do gin and tonic. How refined of you!" Juanita teased, shoving her best friend through the door and towards the Uber driver's car.

"Oh, shut up!"

Both girls were laughing all the way to the car where they were greeted by a friendly brunette who must have been in her mid-20s.

"Wow, I wish I was going out with you two and not heading over to babysit my niece!" the driver laughed and introduced herself, "2 Cats Cocktail Lounge – do I have that right?"

"Absolutely!" Deepika responded, and then added, "Hey, feel free to come by after your niece is taken care of. Knowing us, we'll be there for a while!"

The driver laughed and then sighed, "Oh, I wish. Believe me. This is an overnight gig, unfortunately."

Deepika and Juanita spent the rest of the drive chatting with Katerina. They even exchanged contact information. She seemed nice enough, and they figured maybe they would have a drink with her some time. It turned out that she had just graduated from U of T two years ago and was working at a public school. She'd also had a really rough time with an ex-boyfriend, a talk which prompted Deepika to ask again if she'd like that drink later tonight.

"I'd love to, girls. Another time, for sure!" Katerina pulled up outside the hip bar, "Have fun tonight!"

Deepika and Juanita waved goodbye to their new friend and headed into the lounge. It was dimly lit, and there was a decently large crowd around the bar. It was large enough for the two girls to feel they had picked a good time to go out, but not overwhelming. Deepika took in the atmosphere, and she liked it. It was the right kind of classy, a bit formal but not pretentious. They even had Ed Sheeran playing at the moment. She was sold on the place. All of a sudden, Juanita nudged Deepika in the ribs, taking her completely by surprise, as she'd been humming the tune in her head.

"Ow! What was that for?" Deepika scowled at her friend.

She wasn't scowling for long. She looked in the direction her friend was focused on, and sure enough, she caught sight of the incredibly handsome William Moreau leaning over the bar waiting for what looked like…yes, a beer. Stella Artois. Of course. That was Deepika's favourite beer too. He was wearing a sky blue plaid shirt, tucked into black jeans, and finished off with a sleek black belt with a silver clasp. He had gotten a haircut, Deepika noticed. He'd gotten a smart-looking layered cut and had used a bit of gel to part his dark brown hair to the right. She wouldn't mind running her hands through it…she blushed when she realized that she'd been staring, but he looked incredibly sharp with the top two buttons of his shirt undone and well-maintained stubble enhancing his facial features that it was hard to look away.

"Are you just gonna stare at him, or are you gonna go and say hi to your man?" Juanita hit her friend playfully, "I mean *bonsoir…voulez-vous coucher avec moi?*"

Deepika burst into laughter at the incredibly inappropriate question her friend had proposed she ask, "You are terrible. You know that?" She could feel her cheeks heating up, nevertheless. Part of her wanted him that way, she couldn't deny it. She was 21 years old, and she'd been kissed maybe once or twice, but it was never anything serious. It was perfectly natural for her to want more, but she couldn't just throw herself at him, despite how funny Juanita might find it. She shook her head and told Juanita that she needed to relax before she walked towards William.

"You love it!" Juanita called after her friend as she made her way to the bar.

"Bon soir, Monsieur Moreau," Deepika smiled, as she touched William's shoulder lightly.

He turned to look at her and grinned, "Ah, quelle belle surprise! Bon soir, Madame Kaur. How are you?" He pulled Deepika in for a hug. It lasted longer than she would have expected, but she couldn't deny the fact that she wished it had been longer. His cologne smelled like leather and whiskey, probably the expensive kind. She could have kissed his neck just then, but she controlled herself. The few drinks she had had at home with her best friend and the atmosphere of this bar combined with the fact that she was in William's arms, all of it was getting to her, so she'd pulled away when she'd felt him loosening his grip.

"I'm out with Juanita. She is right over…" Deepika turned around only to find that Juanita was on the other side of the bar chatting with some girls she'd just met, probably hitting on them too, "There."

Deepika and William laughed together. He bought her a drink, and Deepika found out that William's friend had to cancel last minute. She asked him to join her and Juanita in the lounge area to which he quickly acquiesced.

"Hey, Dee," William pulled her aside gently before walking over to the table Juanita had snagged, "You look beautiful."

Deepika melted at his kind words, but she could see the sincerity in his eyes. She smiled and said, "Thank you. You don't look too bad yourself." She winked and turned around, leaving him breathless.

Whoa. Where did that come from? Deepika was surprised at herself. She didn't expect to wink at him. She turned around and saw that he was still standing there with a huge smirk on his face.

"You coming?" she called, and then walked towards Juanita with a confidence that surprised her.

"Damn, girl," Juanita whispered before William could make his way over, "That was pretty amazing…and you've only had a couple of drinks!"

Deepika laughed, "I have no idea where that came from."

The three of them spent the first half of the night joking around. As the night progressed and the drinks kept flowing, Deepika couldn't help but bear her soul. She knew it could be a fault sometimes, to talk too much, but she trusted William and Juanita so she let it out. She told them how she missed her father dearly, but also wasn't sure she could see him at that place. It would break her. Juanita offered to go with her, but Deepika insisted that she would have to see her father alone.

"Dee, see your father. It might make the whole thing he is going through more bearable," William smiled, taking Deepika's hand and giving it an affectionate rub.

"I know," Deepika sighed, "You're both right. It was very hard for me to be around him after his DUI, but you're right. He's trying, and thankfully for him, no one got hurt."

"Hey, come on, this was supposed to be a fun night," William nudged Deepika playfully and draped his arm around her shoulder. She leaned against him and smiled.

"I freaking love this song!" Juanita shouted, interrupting the intimate moment between William and Deepika, "Oh my god, sorry…I didn't mean to be so loud!"

Deepika couldn't contain her laughter at this point, so she shouted back, "You're still being loud!"

Of course the song Juanita was getting so excited about was *Total Eclipse of the Heart*, a classic. Just as Deepika was about to ask William if he wanted to dance, one of the girls Juanita had been chatting up at the bar approached them and told Juanita that she couldn't help but overhear that she loved this song and proceeded to ask her if she'd like to dance. William chuckled with Deepika as they watched Juanita grab the gorgeous blonde's hand and rush to the dance floor.

"Madame?" William held out his hand and added, "S'il vous plaît."

Deepika felt her cheeks heat up at his request but collected herself promptly, "Of course."

They slow-danced near Juanita and her partner. Deepika knew she was already deeply infatuated with William. She wasn't sure about love. But really, was anyone? Any uncertainty she may have had about his sincerity vanished when he offered to drive her to the Bellwood treatment centre whenever she wanted to see her father. He'd wait outside for her, so that she could see him alone. Even though the two of them were somewhat intoxicated, every emotion Deepika felt for this man was real.

"Hey," Deepika said softly, before reaching up to stroke William's cheek with her thumb, "Thank you. For everything."

He caught her hand before she could drop it and smiled, "Any time."

They stood smiling at each other for a while before William called an Uber to take them all home. Juanita rested her head on Deepika's shoulder on the car ride back.

"I'm going to have a killer hangover tomorrow," Juanita mumbled, "Wonderful."

William glanced down at Deepika and chuckled softly. She rested her head on his shoulder and closed her eyes, taking in all the love she felt tonight. How wonderful it was, to have such caring friends, she thought, before drifting into a lucid slumber.

Chapter 10

"Mr. Jha!" the Admissions Counsellor's penetrating voice invaded Jitendra's room and prompted him to slam both hands against his ears to block out the noise. Barbara persisted of course. This was routine, "Jeet, I know you're in there. It's time for breakfast, and then we have the regular group session. Ten minutes, Mr. Jha, please don't be late!"

Wow, she must have to deal with more difficult clients than me if she still manages to maintain that annoyingly optimistic tone twenty-four seven, Jitendra thought, as he threw his pillow across the room in frustration.

"I hate it here," he muttered to himself before getting up and changing into clean clothes. He glanced at his watch and pulled out his iPod shuffle for five minutes of bliss. Lenny Kravitz' *Fly Away* hit his ears and he was on a sandy beach sipping a pina colada.

July 2007. Jitendra had booked a surprise vacation to the Dominican Republic for Asha and Deepika to celebrate a new contract he had signed with a big client. He wasn't much for hanging around on resorts. He'd much rather spend his time at a sports bar or on the golf course, but he knew that his twelve-year old daughter would enjoy the beach, and it had been a while since they had taken some time off as a family. When he had told Ash a day before the flight departed, she was ecstatic. Two days into the trip, and both Ash and Dee were equally happy to lie on the beach and read. Jitendra had bought Dee a lime green iPod Nano a few months ago. As he lay sipping some exotic semi-frozen coconut and rum concoction, which he had to admit, was surprisingly delicious, he remembered how much Dee had cried after she'd found out that all her playlists had been erased after failing to transfer them to the iPod. She had been so immersed in the playlist-making process, every mood of hers with a matching track list, that when she unplugged the iPod from the computer, ready to listen to her brilliant work, she couldn't fathom that a glitch had erased everything. Jitendra chuckled now while he watched his daughter bob her head to Miley Cyrus no doubt – she was the latest and greatest in pre-teen vogue.

"Dad, can I get a drink?" Deepika had taken her earphones out and was sitting up on the lounger. She was eyeing the slushy in her father's hand.

Jitendra laughed and pulled out a five-dollar bill, "Sure, it's right over there." He pointed to the bar.

"What's that one called?" she pointed at the drink in his hand.

Jitendra chuckled, "You can't have this one, but try a Shirley Temple. You'll like it."

Deepika huffed as she stood up and then said, "Fine. Thanks."

Asha looked over from her lounger and laughed with Jeet, "You'd better give her a sip at least. You know our daughter – she'll find out the name and order one tomorrow!"

Both parents burst into a fit of laughter as they recalled how clever their daughter could be when she wanted something. Deepika came back grinning with a Shirley Temple in hand and joked, "I got the spiked version."

"Yeah right!" Jitendra laughed, throwing his daughter a look of disbelief.

"I'm dead serious, Dad."

Jitendra squinted a bit and looked at Deepika a bit longer before she finally stopped stifling the giggles that were bound to escape her. She pointed at her father and bellowed, "You should have seen your face, Dad! I mean seriously…I don't drink alcohol. Come on!"

Jitendra's eyes softened when he figured out that Deepika was joking around and of course was unable to carry the joke for more than thirty seconds. He laughed with his wife and daughter and remembered the many times Deepika had told them that she had gotten a C in one of her courses only to find that she'd received an A about ten seconds into the joke. She was unable to lie about anything, even if it was for humorous purposes. It was a good thing, Jitendra thought to himself, even if it meant that she would always tell him the cold, hard truth.

"Oh, Mr. Jha! Breakfast is now being served!" Barbara's shrill voice interrupted Jitendra's time on the beach and brought him back to a horrid reality.

70

It had hardly been a week at Bellwood, and he was miserable. The people here were too optimistic and over-the-top for him. The routine was ridiculous. Waking up a 8 AM for breakfast, then some stupid meditation session, followed by group counselling. What he needed after this dreadful experience was individual therapy with a man named Johnny Walker. *Shit*, he thought. He still thought of alcohol as a remedy when he knew he was supposed to see it as a plague, something that destroys. He rubbed his eyes and cursed under his breath when Barbara knocked on the door extra loudly this time.

"Coming, coming," Jitendra said in an incredibly monotone voice.

"Mr. Jha, lovely," Barbara beamed at him, "Good morning! You know where to go."

"Yes, thank you. Good morning," Jitendra forced a smile and walked down the hall to the breakfast area.

"Will I be seeing you at meditation this morning, Mr. Jha?" Barbara called after him.

Jitendra turned around and replied sarcastically, "That depends – will Jack Daniels be attending?"

Barbara suppressed the smile that was forming on her lips and shook her head. Jitendra Jha was probably one of the wittiest clients she had ever dealt with at the rehab centre. He was also one of the most difficult ones, but humour was a great coping mechanism for some people. She simply smiled and reminded him, "Remember what we discussed on Tuesday, Jeet. The more you talk about it, the harder it's going to be to let go. Works that way for a lot of things!"

Jitendra laughed and gave Barbara a thumbs up before turning back around and heading to the table for breakfast. There were three long dining tables in front of him. He liked to pick the quietest of the three, every single time. He had no desire to socialize at this hour. He took a seat by an unfamiliar man who was busy drinking black coffee and reading the paper. The man's attention shifted from the news to Jitendra as soon as he felt someone's presence next to him. *Please don't speak,* Jitendra thought. As if the man had read Jitendra's thoughts, he gave him a small smile and a slight nod of the head and then returned to the paper without a word. Jitendra let out a small sigh of relief and then grabbed his daily coffee, toast, and scrambled eggs. This breakfast was useless compared to what he got at home. He would make his espresso steaming hot with the new machine he had purchased, Asha would make omelettes and bacon with the perfect amount of seasoning, and sometimes Deepika would join them in the early mornings and would attempt to discuss politics with him despite her lack of passion for the subject. Here he just hoped no one would speak to him. If Ash hadn't slipped his iPod shuffle into his suitcase, he'd probably have left by now. It was horrible. They were all sheep, just following these counsellors around all day, doing meditation – as if that helped! All he could think about during meditation was going back home, propping himself in front of the TV, and pouring himself a glass of whiskey.

"Mr. Jha! Is a Mr. Jha present? Oh yes, there you are!" an irritating voice disrupted Jitendra's melancholia. He glanced up to see one of the receptionists looking at him excitedly. *Oh god, now what,* he frowned. The receptionist looked ridiculous with that big grin on her face, but she kept gesturing for him to come over so he rolled his eyes and got up. He followed her into the lobby area with his head bowed slightly and his hands in his pocket. He didn't know what to expect, nor was he pleased with the fact that he hadn't gotten to finish his coffee.

He was about to ask what the matter was when he heard a soft, yet clear voice call, "Dad?"

It couldn't be. He shut his eyes tightly and before looking up to make sure that he wasn't hallucinating due to withdrawal. Sure enough, when he glanced up from the ground, he saw his daughter standing just a metre away from him. She was wearing a deep red sweater and dark blue jeans. Her head was tilted to the left as she examined him. That meant she was worried. He snapped out of his trance and strode over to Deepika to hug her. Deepika was taken by surprise at first and didn't know what to do with her arms, but when she saw a tear roll down her father's cheek, she hugged him back. She hadn't ever seen him cry other than when she had picked him up from the police station after his DUI. She also hardly ever experienced this kind of physical affection from her father. Jitendra Jha did not display such deep emotions openly on a regular basis. She had to coax her father into hugs most of the time, and today, when she'd expected him to smile and nod when she first came in, he'd surprised her. She couldn't imagine how hard an experience

72

like this would be for anyone. She couldn't go a day without either talking to her mother, even if it was a brief text message, or her best friend. Once Jitendra had calmed down enough, he let go of Deepika and just looked at her. She smiled at him, but didn't say anything. His eyes told her everything. It was horrible. He hated it, and he wanted to go home.

"You can't give up so soon, Dad," Deepika told him after they had moved to the edge of one of the breakfast tables and ate together. Barbara had given him special permission to skip meditation after Deepika had called in and told her that this would do him more good than any meditation class.

"I know," Jitendra sighed, gulped down his now cold coffee, and then added, "Especially after what I did."

Deepika wasn't about to make him feel worse about his actions even though what he said was completely true. If he gave up after a week of rehab after putting people's lives at risk, she wasn't sure if she could ever speak to him again. He'd have to try harder than that.

"I know you regret what you've done, Dad," Deepika said, reassuring him with a small smile and a gentle pat on his arm, "But you and I both know it's easy to regret with words. Prove to yourself that you genuinely want to fix this. I know you can."

Jitendra nodded and smiled at his daughter and simply said, "It's so good to see you. You have no idea how much I hate this place."

Deepika laughed, "Oh, I have an idea. It was all over your face when you walked into the lobby!"

The two of them joked around and laughed together for the next half an hour. Jitendra was deflecting quite a bit, which disappointed Deepika at some points in the conversation because it was typical of him. She would encourage him, tell him that he could do it, and he wouldn't agree with her. He would drive the conversation in an entirely different direction or stay quiet. She was frustrated because to her, his silence was a sign of a lack of belief in himself. She did enjoy talking to him about normal stuff, things that had nothing to do with rehab or alcohol or the DUI, but she was trying so hard to get through to him and felt that her efforts were being put to waste.

"What's wrong?" Jitendra asked, when there was a break in the conversation.

Deepika didn't want this to end badly, nor did she want to start a fight with her father so she just twiddled her thumbs and replied, "Nothing. Everything's fine. I've told you everything I have to say."

Jitendra smiled, not bothering to probe further. He took her answer at face value and didn't think there was anymore to wonder about. He caught sight of Barbara in the corner of his eye gesturing to him and tapping her watch. It was time for them to wrap it up. Deepika noticed that his attention was elsewhere and turned around to see Barbara waiting.

"Are they always so damn strict around here?" Deepika joked, knowing that it would make her dad laugh. She was right.

"Try living here!" he replied, enjoying the funny exchange. His daughter was all grown up. It was incredible to see. He spoke softly before bidding her farewell and said, "Thank you for coming, Dee. And thank you for telling me about your new friend, and school, and Juanita. I really enjoyed it."

Deepika simply smiled and nodded and stood up to leave. Before she could head towards the exit, Jitendra stopped her.

"I promise I will try my best."

That was all she wanted to hear, and he knew it. He wanted to say that from the start of the conversation, but it took him a while to build up the courage to say it because he knew that with his daughter, he should only say things he meant. That was why he didn't tell her that he promised he would complete the program, or that he would get through this. He told her that he would try his best, and he knew she would hold him to that.

Deepika wiped away a tear that had been dying to fall since she saw her father's state in the lobby and then hugged him tightly, "You haven't seen the last of me, Dad."

"Good," he whispered, trying his best not to choke on tears. She shouldn't see him like that.

A few minutes later, Jitendra was back at the breakfast table alone. Or so he thought. The man he had noticed earlier finally looked up from his paper for a second time and looked at Jitendra and said, "That's quite a daughter you've got. Hold on to that, and I guarantee you'll make it through this hell."

Jitendra smiled back at the stranger, and although he seemed like the kind of man Jitendra might actually have a chance of connecting with, he was too emotional to strike up a conversation at the moment and simply responded with a quick thank you. Outside the Bellwood centre, Deepika was walking towards William Moreau's silver Acura MDX and wiping her eyes simultaneously. As soon as William saw her, he turned off his music and got out of his car. He didn't bother saying anything because he knew that's not what she needed. He just wrapped his arms around her waist and held her against him and whispered that she was amazing for having gone to see her father.

"I'm sure he knows just how lucky he is to have a daughter like you," William spoke softly once Deepika had gotten into the passenger seat.

"Thank you for taking me. I don't know if I could have come alone," she responded, stroking the hand that he'd left resting on the gearshift as he drove.

"Like I said, and like I will continue to say," William looked at her before exiting the parking lot, "Any time."

Deepika smiled at him and then refocused her attention onto the road in front of them. It was long and sometimes the potholes could take them off-guard, but she knew that she had all the support she needed and she would make sure her father got it too. That was the only way they were going to get through this.

END OF PART I

PART II: DEEPIKA KAUR

Chapter 1

It was a crisp October morning, Friday to be exact. Fridays were Deepika's favourite, not because the weekend awaited, although she couldn't deny the excitement she felt at the prospect of no classes, but rather, because her favourite class took place bright and early at 9:30 AM each Friday. Canadian Literature with Dr. Parker, but he preferred Dr. P, because that's what he'd gone by for years. Deepika couldn't decide whether it was the course content that made this her favourite class or Dr. P's charisma and enthusiasm for the darkest of texts. She was equally fond of Molière, Camus, and Dumas from her French classes, but there was something about the way her English professor commanded the room. He never had a problem with students texting in the middle of his class because the ones that were prone to floating off into another world that strayed from Atwood's Ithaca, or Barbara Gowdy's 1960s America because he knew that it was really their loss, not his. Most of the time, the students who attended his class did not text because it was nearly impossible not to be captivated by his passion.

Dr. Parker was one of those professors who refused to remain glued to the podium in the lecture hall. He would make his way from one side to the other, a relaxed sort of pacing back-and-forth, with an obvious intent: to keep students' eyes on him and ears fully engaged. Sometimes he would even walk up the stairs to reach the shy students sitting near the back, just so he could familiarize himself with the cohort he had been assigned. *Now, I am assuming most of you took this class because you wanted to, not because your parents all sat down to give you a talk about how studying Canadian Literature will eventually lead to a lucrative career,* Dr. P had said this during Deepika's very first class of the term, eliciting an uproar of laughter from a senior class of students who had been through three years of questioning from every possible relative regarding their plans for the future. *Yes, it is all quite humorous, but never underestimate the value of a solid liberal arts education. You will learn more about yourself in this classroom than you may think or intend to learn.* He had been completely right. It had only been a month into the term, but Deepika had found inspiration for her own creative writing projects, had realized that she was more confident, and rightfully so, than she had initially believed. She owed a lot to

Dr. Parker and his Canadian Literature class, so when she had told him about her having to leave midway for the selective exchange program to France, he had smiled and said, *Don't let the French make you forget your Canadian roots, Deepika!* They had both laughed in his office, just before he'd officially congratulated her and said that he would make the appropriate arrangements. He then admitted that he was a big fan of French Literature and hoped to hear more about it upon her return in the second term.

The program began in just over a week, so this Friday was one of Deepika's last classes. She had to make it count. Her alarm went off at 6 A.M., and she awoke with a start from an unusually pleasant dream. She was used to either nightmares or nothingness, so when she woke up to delightful images from last night replaying in a loop in her head, she cursed her bloody alarm clock for interrupting her wonderful reverie.

She'd been in France, with Juanita and William. They were sitting on a patio in Nice sipping some form of sparkling Chardonnay. She had no idea of the details, which was true to reality, because for Deepika, as long as the wine was white and sparkling, she enjoyed it. It didn't matter if it was a ten dollar bottle or a sixty dollar one, she wouldn't know the difference if her life depended on it. She couldn't recall the details of the dream – what the conversation had been, which restaurant they'd picked, or what they had ordered. All that she could remember, and it made her all jittery inside, was that she was with her boyfriend in the middle of France, enjoying the cool breeze, gazing at the coast, and probably making inappropriate jokes with Juanita about which French guy her friend would seduce next. Thoughts of this dream turning into a reality in just a few days, combined with the fact that they were discussing Barbara Gowdy's short story "Disneyland" today in class, propelled Deepika towards her bathroom in a fit of excitement.

Thirty minutes tops. That's how long it took Deepika to shower, straighten her hair, put on a light shade of lipstick, and grab her books and computer for class. There were still remnants of her dream drifting around in her head, causing her to pick up her cell phone and call one of her favourite people. Before she could dial, she glanced at her bedside clock and realized that she was getting too late to talk on the phone if she wanted to grab her daily Americano Misto from the Starbucks around the corner before she got to class.

Her father used to order that drink every day before dropping her off to school. She got used to hearing his order each morning, so much so, that one day in high school, she repeated the same order, with her father's confidence despite not knowing what exactly the drink consisted of. She smiled as she remembered drinking it without any added sugar to give off the same air of sophistication her father did when he sipped the coffee at his office desk in his crisp grey jacket and pristine white shirt finished with denim jeans and a simple black belt. No tie, though. Ties were reserved for business meetings only. Now, she walked into the Starbucks, located on College Street and just a ten-minute walk from campus, that she came to frequent ever since her second year at the University of Toronto.

The line wasn't too bad, thankfully. Deepika glanced at her silver watch, noting that it was a few minutes past 7 A.M. William was supposed to meet her for coffee at this Starbucks shortly. They had made it a routine. Every Friday, they would have a coffee together before their classes because they'd only see each other in one class a week, Deepika's introductory French Literature class. She would get a grande Americano Misto almost every single time. He would either get an Americano and take it straight or get a French Roast with a bit of milk. *Of course*, Deepika had laughed when they'd had their first-ever coffee date in September. *What, you aren't going to get a chai tea latté?* William had teased her because he knew that the redundancy of that drink's name bugged her. Deepika suppressed giggles at the memory and was about to grab her drink when a familiar silvery voice greeted her, *Bonjour, ma chérie.*

They sat down at their table, the small one by the window. It was positioned perfectly. Just enough sunlight came through that morning, enough so that the rays hit William's face at the right angles, accentuating his gorgeous features – those dark long lashes, the chocolate brown layers of wavy hair that he'd gelled just enough to give him a clean, attractive look, and that well-maintained facial hair of his that she loved to run her fingers and lips over while sitting in his lap on lazy Sundays. His handsome face in the sun and that tiny hint of a smile that never left his lips would mesmerize Deepika to the point where she would trail off in the middle of her outpouring of emotion because she was busy imagining them walking the *Champs Elysées* just before the sun set. He was now able to tell when this was happening and would just smirk at her and laugh, *I know I'm handsome, but I didn't know I had hypnotic powers,* to which Deepika would snap out of her trance and playfully slap the hand that would inch closer to hers in an attempt to make her swoon further.

"Really, tell me, how's your Dad?" William interrupted her romantic thoughts of him and turned to a more serious topic.

Deepika sighed, not particularly interested in talking about that after what her mother had sent her in the mail, but his smile was so warm, his eyes so concerned, that she couldn't help but tell him everything. Asha had sent her a letter a few days ago. It was very much to the point, like most of her letters, but this one felt different. Deepika hardly felt any comfort reading the last few words, *Believe me; he is trying,* because the rest of the letter had been so upsetting. It was as disappointing as receiving subpar grades on a paper one had worked tirelessly on, with two or three lines of encouragement on the back of it. They meant nothing when the reality was that it simply wasn't good enough. *You'll do better next time.* Her father doesn't get a *next time,* Deepika thought. This is it. This is the final exam. There are no comments at the end, no second chances. She felt like the ruthless invigilator at one of her university finals. *You have two hours to complete the exam. No exceptions. No cheating.* Maybe she was too young and childish to keep herself from judging her father. Who did he think he was? He thought he could drive under the influence, go to rehab for three weeks, and then tell his counsellor that he wanted to leave? He thought that he could say that he had tried, and that his daughter and wife would welcome him home with open arms and watch him kill himself every night until there was nothing left but a limp skeleton in his chair by the television that he loved so much.

She was mad at herself for being so harsh. She scolded herself for her lack of empathy because she was supposed to be happy for him just for enrolling in the program. She was supposed to stay and support him even if he dropped it in a week. The problem with empathy, she thought, was that people assumed that it was infinite, that people could hurt you a million times but you would understand because you had an endless supply of *it's okays* and hugs to give. At some point even the most caring of people get tired, and if people like her father could use the argument that he was only human, then people like herself should be able to say the same thing.

She was tired of giving five hundred percent to people who gave her ten percent back. The rate of return was not worth the investment. She knew that. But deep down, she also knew that she would never be able to stop caring. She'd tried it, this one time after she had gotten into a big argument with her father. She'd tried to ignore him, give him the silent treatment. She had managed to go a day without speaking to him or acknowledging his presence, but the second she saw the slightest hint of pain in his expression or hurt in his eyes, even if her imagination was making her see what she wanted to, she'd break. How was she supposed to ever teach anyone a lesson, if she kept going back because she loved him or her so much?

"Hey," William's soft voice stopped her in the middle of her self-loathing, "Since when is caring too much a fault?"

Deepika smiled at his attempt to comfort her, but she knew how much of a fault it could be based on the number of times she'd been hurt. She'd been hurt by her father, although may have been genuinely oblivious to it for the past few years up until the DUI, and by this boy she loved back in high school. She didn't know how to find a middle ground. If she loved someone, every part of her displayed that affection to the point where she scared people. It was too raw, too emotional for some people. They couldn't handle the purity of her feelings, or something like that. She couldn't remember the wording Juanita had used when she cried over that boy, but her friend had told her over and over again that one day, someone is going to appreciate your honesty and your love, like she did. Don't give it to people who don't deserve it, she'd said. Deepika had been dating William Moreau for less than a month, but he seemed to understand her in a way that no one else did. Maybe it was the fact that he was young, like her, and had these ideas about love that hadn't been tarnished deeply enough for him to turn cold. Or maybe, he had the same fire in his heart, that no matter how many people tried to extinguish with their harsh words and disbelief, would continue to burn even if it eventually consumed him too.

"Seriously, Dee," William continued when she didn't respond, "You speak as though having as warm of a heart as yours is a flaw. Sure, Juanita is right, don't give so much of yourself to people who don't deserve it. But listen to me, anyone would be lucky to be touched with your kindness, with your genuine heart, for a month, for a day, for even a single moment. They are lucky. They don't have to admit that, but trust me when I say, they know."

Deepika reached over to squeeze his hand and smiled, "How did you find me, Moreau?"

William grinned at Deepika's endearing use of his last name, and the hopeless romantic in him spoke, "Hearts that beat the same find each other, no doubt."

Any other day, Deepika would have rolled her eyes at the cheesy comment, but this morning she let it sink in. She didn't want to give every part of herself to him too fast because she was scared it wouldn't work out, but she knew deep down, that he already had her heart. She could have stayed there in that Starbucks with him all day, but she had class to attend, and she was certain that the staff would give her dirty looks if she didn't dish out eight bucks every few hours for a large drink to make up for occupying their comfortable couches. Just as she was about to check her watch, her phone buzzed, reminding her that she needed to start walking to campus. William heard it and threw her a knowing, yet wistful look. She smiled back at him, kissed him quickly, and headed out the door into the cool autumn weather. Bundling her scarf into her black H&M coat, she buttoned it up, and stuck her earphones into her ear. She pulled her iPhone out of her pocket, hit shuffle, and within seconds, Eva Cassidy's rendition of "Autumn Leaves" entered her ears and floated into her subconscious, and her thoughts began to swirl like the leaves, the deep reds and burgundies, carried by the wind.

"Damn it!" Deepika slammed her fists onto her lap. She was trying to learn the piano solo portion of the classic jazz tune, "Autumn Leaves".

She wanted to play it for Christmas dinner. They were having friends over, and everyone always asked her to play something, and she wanted this piece to be the one. Her mother had parent-teacher interviews and had gone to bed early out of sheer exhaustion, and her father was not home yet. He went to visit one of his friends, and generally, when that happened, he wasn't home until midnight. Deepika groaned at the thought of having to open the door to a piss drunk father who would be struggling to take his shoes off, let alone make his way upstairs without some help. *Just watch,* Deepika thought, *this time I'll leave him passed out on the couch.* A minute after thinking that, she shook her head and mumbled, "Yeah right." Sometimes she wondered if she had a mild form of saviour complex because it didn't seem to matter how angry her father made her, she could never bring herself to hate him. She'd curse him in her bedroom when he did something stupid, scream that she hated him, although she had recently turned to writing as a means of expression because she figured the yelling just got her into more shit. But at the end of it all, she didn't believe half the words she said about him. Deepika took a deep breath, drank some water, and tried the solo once more. Somehow, she managed to play it through error-less. It sounded like the recording!

"Perfecto!" Deepika rejoiced, packing her books away triumphantly. Unfortunately, the sound of a taxi pulling into the driveway and the proceeding noise of the doorbell interrupted her momentary happiness at the achievement. Her expression turned upset; she couldn't mask it with a fake smile. She glared through the window as she walked past it to see her father grinning like a fool. One more exaggerated sigh and a sarcastic *here we go* later, she opened the door slowly to let her father in.

"Where's Mom?" he asked, completely oblivious to the fact that both Deepika and her mother had told him that she had interviews and would be tired when she got home.

"Sleeping, obviously," Deepika was annoyed, and then she added, "She actually works on Fridays."

Jitendra didn't catch the personal attack Deepika had thrown at him because he was stumbling around trying to find the light. She sighed again, totally used to this, and turned on the light.

"What's for dinner?" Jitendra asked, with that same stupid look on his face, as though he could show up near midnight and everyone would be waiting to greet him even when he couldn't speak coherently.

Deepika was past the point of annoyance, so she angrily responded, "Normal families eat dinner together every night at bloody seven o' clock, not fucking midnight with their drunk father!"

Now, she had her father's attention. He was stunned at her free use of bad language in front of him. It was as though he had sobered up within seconds of hearing that. His expression turned stern and he narrowed his eyes at his daughter, "Don't ever use that word with me again."

Deepika was so angry that she pushed him even further. Something had taken over her and she couldn't control it, even though she could see that her father was getting very upset.

"What? Drunk? You don't like that word?" Deepika continued, "Try living with one." She didn't wait for him to respond. She stalked up to her room, locked her bedroom door, and plopped onto her bed. She had a small balcony from which she could she the front door and foyer area, so she peeped through the windowed door and saw her father stumble towards the television room, presumably to sleep on the couch with the TV running in the background. Deepika was too frustrated with Jitendra to sit and cry, so she pulled out her journal and recorded the events that had occurred that day and the past few days. December 20, 2015. She scribbled furiously every curse word that came to mind, and ended with *I can't wait to go back to school.*

Deepika didn't cry when she recalled that horrible night during last year's winter holidays. She simply remembered it. She had forgiven her father, but she could not forget. Forgetting was dangerous. It could make people believe that things had changed.

Deepika walked into the Jackman Humanities Building where her class was being held. Her music stopped momentarily, so she pulled her phone out to see what had happened. Her frown disappeared instantly when she saw a text from her boyfriend light up the black screen: *Have fun in class, don't worry so much!* He'd added a little monkey emoticon next to the text to make her laugh, she was certain. She typed a quick response because she saw her professor walk through the double doors with his classic black trench coat, books in one hand, and a large Tim Horton's coffee in the other. She smiled at her instructor and made her way into the classroom.

"Hey Deepika, how's it going?" Dr. Parker asked just as he reached the doors to the lecture hall.

"It can only be going well when I've got this class!" Deepika laughed.

Her professor chuckled as he held the door open for a few students and gestured for her to go inside as well, "Ready to go to Disneyland?"

Deepika smiled at the reference to today's lecture material and replied wittily, "Only if I get to stay."

Chapter 2

Deepika admired her efficient packing skills as she reached over her suitcase to zip up the belongings she would require for the next three months. It felt as though she had been sitting in her Can. Lit. class just minutes ago, and now she was preparing for her flight to Nice with her best friend.

"Wow, looks like you're all set," Asha smiled, as she entered her daughter's bedroom. Of course Deepika had come home for the weekend before flying out. She wasn't going to leave her mother with just a phone call. She had seen her father last week but didn't have the chance to see him that weekend because she'd gone home. Deepika caught sight of her mother's watery eyes and walked over to wrap her arms around her mother's waist.

"It's only for a couple of months, Mom," Deepika reassured her, "Plus I'll be perfectly safe with Juanita, you know that."

Asha laughed, "I don't know about her. She's a little crazy, that one!"

"I heard that!" Juanita bounded into Deepika's bedroom and hugged her friend's mother, "I'm not *that* insane, Mrs. Kaur!"

Asha had her arms around both her daughter and the girl she treated like her own. She couldn't have been happier to have them at home with her before they had to leave the next morning.

"I don't know, Mrs. Kaur, she's pretty sketchy," a husky voice interrupted the moment between the girls.

Deepika immediately turned to see William join them and couldn't contain the excitement she knew was visible on her face when he smirked at her and said, "Hello, sweetheart."

"William!" Deepika exclaimed, as she embraced him tightly. He'd told her that he might not be able to see her until a few weeks into the trip, and yet, there he was standing in her bedroom along with her mother and best friend. The only one missing was her father. A twinge of pain hit her as she remembered how happy he had been when she stopped by the last time. He should've been with them right now, making jokes and sipping on his favourite scotch. She felt bad instantly and made a mental note to call him that night. Having her boyfriend with her made her feel a bit better, so she chose not to dwell on the isolation her father must have been feeling this evening.

"Now this boy," Asha began, giving William a hug once Deepika had let go of him, "He's definitely going to take care of my daughter." She knew Juanita would fire back immediately and tried to suppress the laugh that attempted to force its way out of her mouth.

"Excuse me!" Juanita screeched, "I have, what, a decade on you, buddy? This guy is still in the testing phase. Two months doesn't cut it with me, Dee!"

They all burst into laughter at Juanita's overly dramatic reaction. Asha had expected nothing less, which made the situation all the funnier. She had taken it upon herself to invite the two of them to stay the night since they were all leaving in the morning. William had requested her not to tell Deepika that he had gotten special permission to travel to France for the first month of the program because he wanted to surprise her. Of course, when he finally divulged this secret to her over gourmet pasta, which Asha had cooked, and wine, that he and Juanita had brought with them, she was ecstatic. She even shared her dream with them, the one in which they are drinking on a patio by the coast, watching sailboats turn into specks as they drifted further away from the shore. Asha sat with the three of them all evening, enjoying the young company. She smiled at the energy they had, their positivity, and their genuine love for each other.

William had been over to their house a few times for dinner ever since he and Deepika had begun dating, and he had even come into the rehab centre with Deepika one day to meet Jitendra. As was typical of her father, he was uncomfortable with the idea of her being in a relationship. He'd spent the hour with William joking around to the point where Deepika started getting upset because he wouldn't be serious about anything, including his unacceptably slow progress. Deep down, she knew that her father was using humour as a defence mechanism. He was embarrassed that his daughter's boyfriend, a complete stranger to him, was visiting him at a rehab centre. He felt so ashamed. He'd rather meet William at home, where he could drill the guy with questions over a couple of beers, where he would be relaxed. It was hard enough being in that rehab centre, and then to have Deepika introduce her boyfriend, and he could see how close the two of them were, well it was a bit too much for Jitendra to handle all at once. Nonetheless, Deepika had done her job. She had introduced William to both her parents, and while she knew her father would take some time to get used to the idea, she was filled with joy at the fact that her mother adored him.

You've found yourself quite the gentleman, Dee, Asha had told her after the three of them had their first dinner together. Asha and Deepika had been sitting on the couch while William cleaned up in the kitchen after insisting that it was the least he could do. There had been a break in the conversation, and then Asha had gathered the courage to ask about what had been concerning her most. She could see, even after just one dinner, how in love her daughter was and how close the two of them truly were. *You're being careful, right?* She had muttered the question under her breath, but asked it unabashedly. Asha's mother had never been one to shy away from the realities of life, no matter how conditioned society had become to accepting taboos as just that – things one should never discuss. Asha had agreed wholly with her mother. The worst thing a parent could do was leave his or her child entirely in the dust about matters that everyone deals with at some point – why not make it easier for them? Deepika had understood her mother's question correctly and couldn't help the small smile that began to creep onto her lips before she had responded, *We just started dating, Mom!* The two of them had definitely had their fair share of heated moments at William's place, but they always took precautions. Sometimes Deepika felt that he was even more careful than she was, and she loved that about him. Deepika and Asha were so close, sometimes Asha was taken aback at just how much her daughter would share with her. Asha valued the comfort her daughter had with her, but despite her general openness, Deepika could be a talkative girl who had a habit of embarrassing her parents with too much information at times. That evening, however, Asha saw a girl who had matured in ways that perhaps Deepika was unaware of. Her response had been brief, playful, but to the point. She was being careful, and that was all Asha needed to know.

Seated by the fire, Asha now watched Deepika punch William's shoulder lightly for teasing her about her singing every time they were in the car. She saw herself in her daughter and remembered the couple of weeks leading to her wedding. The honeymoon phase, getting to know each other before the deep character flaws could surface, she remembered it being a lot of fun.

Then she got married, and the Jitendra Jha that had courted her quickly became overshadowed by a moody, unpredictable alcoholic. The fun-loving joker she had been excited to marry did not completely disappear, however. There were moments between them, similar to what Asha now saw between Deepika and William, which made it all worthwhile. Those small, seemingly insignificant moments perhaps to an outsider, kept Asha in love with Jitendra despite the major issues between them.

"Shit!" Deepika cursed, interrupting Asha's train of thought and causing her to glance up worriedly.

"What's wrong?" Juanita asked concernedly. She glanced between Deepika and Asha quickly.

"I have to call Dad," Deepika responded as she stood up hastily, "Before his hours are over." She glanced at the kitchen clock. It was only 8 P.M. There shouldn't be an issue, plus Barbara had promised Jitendra an extra phone call given the special circumstances surrounding Deepika's trip abroad.

The phone call didn't last long. Jitendra ended it earlier than Deepika had expected, but when she had heard his voice thicken and his speech slow, she knew that he had been overcome with emotion. She too had found it difficult to say goodbye over the phone. She would have much rather gone to the facility to see him in person, but she had chosen to spend the majority of her time with her mother. Her mother was alone in that house and would have to be for another couple of months if Jitendra stuck it out at Bellwood. Little did Deepika know, that despite being surrounded by people, his counsellors and his fellow addicts, Jitendra suffered. He suffered because he was often alone with his thoughts, and his thoughts were not pleasant. They were filled with painful memories from which he had never received even the slightest form of closure, unshared moments that pervaded his nightmares, and a past that he could not escape because he hadn't let himself move on. He feared that if he chose to let go, all that would remain was a deep pit of nothingness. The sorrow and disappointment gave him something to latch onto, something to reflect on to make the time pass faster in both the physical and mental prisons to which he was subject.

The last thing Deepika had said to Jitendra was brief but poignant, and it resonated deeply with him. *Dad, I would never hate you for not being able to complete the program, but I will always love you for trying.* He had to give it his best shot. It had just been a few weeks. He knew that he could do better. He hadn't even tried to make friends, as Deepika had suggested. That would surely make it easier to live in that place. After Deepika had hung up, Jitendra walked back to his room to listen to some music. He sat down at the chair by his desk and scrolled mindlessly through his iPod when he discovered something he hadn't noticed before. When he scrolled all the way to the bottom – he had been listening to the playlist Asha had created for him endlessly – there was another playlist that took him by surprise: Feel-Good Hits - Love Dee.

Deepika had built a playlist for him with modern tracks that she knew he enjoyed. He felt himself begin to smile uncontrollably when he heard John Newman's "Love Me Again" because it took him back to an afternoon where he and Deepika were driving back from the golf course after a 9-hole round ready to have some beer on the patio and barbecue beef patties. The song had begun to play on the radio, and immediately, Jitendra had turned it up and lowered both their windows. He couldn't keep himself from moving in his tiny cubicle of a dorm room. For the first time in years, Jitendra did something that he hadn't done sober since he was a child. He stuffed his iPod in the back pocket of his jeans, and he stood up to dance. He danced without a care in the world. The music got to him. The sound waves entered his outer ear, flowed through the auditory canal, and then ended up in his veins, shocking his heart and bringing him back to life. After going through about half the playlist, he collapsed onto his bed from the physical exertion, but he felt rejuvenated. He would try to make friends tomorrow. He would try.

Chapter 3

The blaring alarm clock programmed to go off each morning at 7 A.M., which each resident was unfortunately forced to keep in his or her room, roused Jitendra from his poor excuse of a sleep. Despite having felt energized and optimistic after listening to his daughter's playlist, his subconscious had taken him elsewhere in his dreams. He sat up groggily and rubbed his eyes as he took in his surroundings again. One would think he'd be used to seeing the tiny desk across from his uncomfortably small twin bed and the shabby closet by the door by the third week of his treatment, but upon sitting up, he squinted as his eyes were hit by the few rays of sunlight coming through the little window, and his mind needed to adjust to the fact that he may be told that his stay was to be extended today. Today was his interim check up with his Admissions Counsellor. He had no clue how Barbara dealt with him, let alone all the other patients that were as stubborn if not worse. She was so bubbly and positive all the time, and while he found it irritating upon first enrolling in the program, he almost loved her for it now. But he would never tell her that, of course. He didn't spend another second thinking about his meeting with Barbara nor the disturbing nightmare he had had. The longer he sat on his bed, the greater the chance that the distressing images would flash continuously in his head. So he stood up quickly, brushed his teeth, threw on a pair of dark blue jeans and a stylish black quarter-zip sweatshirt and headed down for breakfast. Spending too much time in that room alone was scarier than sitting by himself at breakfast. At least there, the chatter from the more talkative residents blocked out the screams from his childhood. His pace quickened as he strode down the hallway to the dining area. *Quickly, before the images invade your head again. Quickly, before you remember it all.*

He was rather grateful to see Barbara greet him and remind him of his appointment time later on in the day just before he got to his seat. He needed to hear voices other than the persistent one in his head that wouldn't shut up. He fixed his eyes on his usual spot and saw that the man who usually sat with his newspaper and coffee was just a couple of seats away. He made up his mind. He was going to attempt to speak to this man; after all, the man seemed like his type of guy. Solitary, thoughtful, and quiet. Perhaps they would get along, or perhaps they would prefer sitting in isolation. Either way, he had promised Deepika that he would at least try. He poured his coffee, grabbed a piece of toast, and sat down with a small sigh. He felt as though he was back in high school, trying to make friends and get that fresh start he had desired after elementary school. For a man who usually found it easy to strike up conversations with total strangers, he struggled to initiate with the man next to him. Was this how his daughter felt when she wanted to talk to him? Was he that unapproachable? The man Jitendra had been hoping to engage in conversation reminded him of his father – cold, reserved, quiet. So uncomfortably quiet…

"I couldn't help but overhear the last time your daughter came to visit," the man holding the paper lowered it to look at Jitendra, who was visibly surprised at the sudden acknowledgment, and then continued, "But is she studying in France?"

Jitendra overcame his momentary shock and responded proudly, "Yes, she is. It's a special exchange program for students interested in French literature."

The man looked intrigued now and had folded up the newspaper so that his attention was focused on Jitendra. He looked a lot older than Jitendra, probably around 65, Jitendra estimated in his head. He had pale skin, a bit of grey hair remaining on his head, and creases by the corner of his eyes when he smiled. He wore rectangular reading glasses, which he had also taken off and slipped into his shirt pocket.

"I'm John, by the way," he held out his hand, and Jitendra shook it after introducing himself as Jeet.

"What are you in for?" Jitendra joked, as he dug into his scrambled eggs and toast, feeling a bit more at ease.

John laughed and replied, "Drinking…too much, apparently. You too?"

Jitendra was smiling now. John seemed like someone he would get along with. He then said, "Yes, Sir. But I really deserve to be here after what I did." The mood turned sombre as Jitendra divulged the story of his DUI, the way in which his daughter and wife had turned their backs on him after finding out, but also the unexpected support he had received and continued to receive, from both.

95

"I really don't deserve it," he said, pushing a piece of egg to the edge of his plate with his fork, his eyes intrigued by the light trail of oil the movement left behind.

"Hey, you're here. You know you fucked up, and that's what counts," John smiled, patting his new acquaintance on the shoulder, before adding, "And no one got hurt physically."

"Physically," Jitendra repeated, pondering the depth of that statement. How had he hurt his wife and daughter emotionally? He remembered something Deepika had said to him once, while he was drunk no doubt. Somehow the words stuck despite his inebriated state. *Physical pain is temporary. The emotional damage you're doing to me will probably last a lifetime. Did you ever consider that?* He cringed as he recalled that harsh truth. He was so selfish, he thought. He had been so self-concerned and self-absorbed, that in order to numb his own emotional distress, he had inflicted more of it onto the two people he loved most in the world. And what had they done to deserve it? They had chosen to love him.

"Sometimes I wonder," John interrupted Jitendra's distressing thoughts as he leaned back in his chair, "Sometimes I wonder if anyone would really miss me if I just called it quits."

Jitendra knew what he meant right away. He'd had this thought before too. It came and went, but it was worse in the winters. Sometimes, it would pain him so much, that in a drunken state, he would thoughtlessly say to his wife that he wanted to end it. Deepika had screamed and cried in the past when he would talk like that, and in the moment he could not understand her reaction, but when John continued to speak about his family, he knew that he did have people who would miss him. It wasn't that he didn't know this before, but there were times in the past where the thought of none of it existing anymore was more powerful than any love Deepika or Asha had for him. He recalled one particular evening when an important business deal had fallen through, his bank had called him regarding a large payment that needed to be made on his line of credit, and neither his wife nor his daughter had been speaking to him. It was moments like that, in which he wondered if anyone would miss him. Moments in which he was sitting alone in his office, the dim lights flickering because they needed to be replaced, and nothing but the sound of the refrigerator whirring in the kitchen. Those were the kinds of unbearably lonely moments in which he couldn't see anything but the black night outside and couldn't find anything worth returning to. He couldn't sit with himself. Maybe that was why he left work early ninety percent of the time. Before the darkness fell, before his employees went back to their families, before the only aggravatingly loud noise was the ringing of his miserable thoughts forcing their way into his already crowded mind. John had been talking despite Jitendra having drifted away for a couple of minutes, but he had heard bits and pieces of it. John was a widower; his only estranged son was working in California at some marketing firm, so he was almost entirely alone. He had a couple of friends, but not one that he missed in the slightest.

"Why are you here, then?" Jitendra asked bluntly, but he was genuinely curious. A man who had nothing, no one to get better for, why would he go through such torture? John's answer caught him off guard. He could not speak, or smile, or look the man in the eyes. This man had something he didn't think he could ever have.

"I'm here for myself," John repeated, calmly. He wore a permanent half-smile on his lips that never seemed to disappear completely. It either became fuller or faded a bit, and Jitendra began to wonder if the man had some sort of condition that made it impossible for him to frown. Either that, or there was some joke that he kept replaying in his mind to keep him smiling like that, Jitendra thought.

"Did I say something to upset you?" John asked concernedly when Jitendra stared at his plate and did not make an effort to continue the conversation.

Jitendra glanced up and shook his head, "No, nothing. I was just thinking." He focused his attention on the blood-red ketchup in the corner of his plate. It remained untouched. The more he looked at it, the deeper the hues of red got, and the more he could not stand the sight. He pushed his plate away, repulsed, and his eyes shifted to his black coffee, which must have been cold by now. The seemingly endless black liquid had a hypnotic effect on him, and slowly, he was sucked into the void and taken to another time.

Jitendra ran frantically through the busy city streets of Chandigarh, glancing all around him as he flitted through intersections. He was trying to locate a pharmacy or anyone who could help him get a package of gauze pads or even a first aid kit. He had less than 50

97

rupees remaining in his pocket, and he had been unable to reach his aunt and uncle because they were not at home and he had no other means of contacting them. His eight-year old sister was at home, hopefully still sitting on the couch with a bloody towel wrapped around her hand. She had been unexpectedly calm when the knife slipped from the wet surface of the cucumbers she had been slicing for salad and left what Jitendra perceived as a horrendously deep cut in the thenar space, the little valley of skin between her precious thumb and index finger. He had jumped to grab a damp towel and had forced his baby sister to sit on the couch, while reassuring her that it wasn't that deep of a nick. He had then lunged into the city streets with all the change he had left in order to find appropriate bandage, and if he was lucky, some form of medical assistance. As he ran, he glanced about him to see if there was anyone who would be able to offer him some extra money to go to the pharmacy or if anyone had medical gauze and disinfectant on him or her. He knew a bit about first aid from school. He knew that he had to stop the bleeding by applying enough pressure, which he hoped his sister was doing at home as he had instructed her to, and he knew that it was important to apply a bit of alcohol to the wound to prevent infections.

He caught sight of a daabawaala walking the streets with his tiffins full of various daals, chicken curries, and naan, no doubt, and approached him desperately, pointing to the man's backpack and asking whether he had any first aid material in it to help control his sister's bleeding. When the man shook his head without a word of where Jitendra may be able to find help, or any sort of well-wishing, Jitendra maintained the decency he had learned in school, said a quick *shukriyaa* and ran to the thelawala with his hope beginning to diminish. He addressed the man, who was preparing pani puri and chaat for the customers in line, politely but hurriedly when he noticed that it had been almost fifteen minutes since he'd left Anita at the house.

"Bhaiya, medical supplies hai? In the restaurant?" he begged the street-food vendor and explained his sister's injury in full, only to be shooed away with nothing but a grunt and a brief gesture at the growing line of customers waiting to stuff their mouths with savoury chickpeas and potatoes with no care for the pre-teen boy who was just trying his best to take care of his little sister. Jitendra was

98

disappointed and couldn't help but wonder why it was that everyone in India addressed their fellow men as *brother* when there was no sense of camaraderie or concern for one another to be found. He dragged his feet disappointedly across the unpaved gravel and tried asking some of the chai-drinkers by the vendor's stand. Some of the women with their young toddlers offered him wet wipes and a few words of encouragement, but not a single one gave him the few more rupees he needed to buy a legitimate kit. He was about to turn back and make do with the few things he had managed to collect when a group of men called him over.

"Oy! Baccha!" they yelled, succeeding in finally getting Jitendra's attention. He turned around to look at a group of large men who seemed to be drunk. Some of them had beer stains on their shirts and remnants of food around their mouths. He was immediately frightened, but the prospect of them having what he needed inclined him to approach them cautiously.

"So you need money?" one of them leaned forward with a wicked smirk on his face.

"Yes, to buy a first aid kit for my sister," he said quickly, trying to gauge whether or not the men were going to help him.

"Oy, Bobby!" the man who had been talking to Jitendra slapped his friend on the shoulder, "He has a sister!"

The men roared with laughter and made crude gestures with their hands. Jitendra had seen enough, so he started to turn and was about to run home when the same man who had asked if he needed money stopped him.

"Bring your sister here, and we will buy your first aid kit," he grinned and then said, "Tell me, is she beautiful?"

The men all cackled maliciously at the comment as their minds pictured taking advantage of this girl one by one. Jitendra knew what they were thinking and was so taken aback and angry that these men were speaking of his younger sister in such a despicable manner, that he swiftly grabbed two of the beer bottles on the table while the pigs were busy discussing their twisted fantasies. Without a second to realize what the little boy had in mind, the animal closest to him cried out in pain when the beer bottle came crashing down onto his crooked head. Before the other men could grab Jitendra, he told them never to dare speak of any girl that way again and then threw the second beer bottle with immense force at one of the men who still wore a disgusting grin, hoping to knock the brute's teeth out. Then he ran, as fast as he possibly could, remembering one of the races he had competed in with his friend in gym class the other day. Something inhuman had taken over, propelling him towards home with anger in his mind and love for his sister in his heart. He ran so fast that he could barely hear those men cursing him from the table they were probably still too drunk to move from. He smiled in satisfaction when he recalled the crimson dripping from the man's head after he had hit him and hoped that the knock to the head would cleanse the man's vile and vicious thoughts from inside.

"Jeet!" Anita ran to her brother as soon as he entered the house again. He hugged her sister and locked the door before helping her with the wound again. Thankfully, it had gotten better, and he was not as worried. While he had been out, Anita told him that Gaurav Uncle and Sunita Aunty had called and were on their way over to treat the wound completely. He breathed a sigh of relief and thought perhaps he should have stayed with his sister and waited instead of risking his safety the way he had. Risking his safety meant that he was risking his sister's as well because she needed him. Jitendra smiled at Anita, made some tea for them as well as their relatives, and sat on the couch with his sister knowing that everything would be just fine. He just needed to wait a while.

"Hey," John shook Jitendra's shoulder lightly and said, "Sorry to disturb the impromptu nap but Barbara's calling you for your interim."

What a way to wake up, Jitendra thought, not realizing that he had inadvertently dozed off at the breakfast table. It turned out that he'd only been out for fifteen minutes, according to John. He thanked his new friend and glanced towards the exit to see Barbara holding a clipboard. She didn't look as overly happy today. That couldn't be good. He exhaled heavily and stood up, headings towards the inevitable.

"Best of luck," John smiled. Jitendra nodded and walked over to his Admissions Counsellor with his insides dreading what she would say.

They were in her office. His file was laid out neatly on her desk with numerous red markings in various categories. Jitendra was used to seeing red markings like that on his tests at school. He hadn't been a fan of studying. He felt like a schoolboy again, waiting for his parents on interview night, only to be disappointed again when his father did not show and his mother came in frantically, late as usual. What was the teacher going to say today? He was in a perpetual state of detention, so how much worse could it get?

"Jitendra, we are going to advise that you spend at least half a month more here on top of the time you have left," Barbara spoke seriously, but a hint of that never-fading smile still remained on her lips, before she added, "We do not recommend the outpatient program. Based on your participation in the counselling sessions, we don't think you are ready for that."

After a long pause, Jitendra spoke up and asked, "You're making me extend my stay by another two weeks?"

Barbara's eyes softened and she smiled, "I'm advising you, Jitendra. You can change your life entirely, it's up to you."

That's what they kept telling him, but the truth was that if it were really up to him, he'd go back to his old lifestyle. He hadn't driven his gorgeous Rover in weeks, he hadn't been able to workout in his home gym or watch the football game with a side of red wine and salted pistachios, and he hadn't been able to hug his beautiful wife or play *Name that Tune* with his intelligent daughter. He hadn't heard his daughter's guitar in what felt like ages, or the mix of English, French, and Spanish music she'd play on the home's sound system. He could only go back to that iPod shuffle for solace so many times, or chat with John over coffee so many mornings, before he lost his mind.

"Hey, but it looks like you're making friends," Barbara interrupted his dismal thoughts, "That's a great sign!"

I miss my friends at home, Jitendra thought. He was loyal and could never replace his core group no matter how nice outsiders were. They did not grow up with him, they did not know his quirks or what really made him tick, and they never would because only a certain special group of people stuck around for so long. Barbara and Jitendra went over the next steps of his treatment, and she advised him to call Asha to let her know. He didn't know if he could go through with that. There was no sound worse than hearing your beloved's voice break over the phone and being unable to console her with your arms. He had to go through with it regardless, so when Barbara left him with the phone, he took a deep breath before dialling the home number he would never forget, for the digits were imprinted on his soul.

Chapter 4

Dear Deepika,

I hope you are having a lovely time in France with your friends. I know I promised you that I would call if there was anything urgent, but I don't have the strength to tell you over the phone. Dad's rehab has been extended for half a month more. He's trying, but progress has been very slow. He isn't opening up during the counselling sessions, and they don't think he'll be ready to go home by the end of the month. He requested the outpatient program, but they don't think he'll be able to control himself if he is not in the centre. Please don't worry about this, Dee. I want you to have a good time, and your father didn't even want me to pass on the message, but I know how angry you'd be if you weren't kept in the loop. I'm sure he'd appreciate a phone call from you whenever you have a chance. I promised you that I'd keep you posted, and I will continue to do so. I am doing well, and I am visiting your father regularly. Keep sending me emails and photos – it's only been a few days, and it looks like you three are having a wonderful time!

Love,
Mom

That was the letter Deepika had received in the morning after one of the roommates on her floor had delivered it to her personally because the mailman had mixed up their rooms. Despite what her mother had written about not worrying, Deepika could not help but feel concerned. It was too early in the morning to call her father, so she made a mental note to do it at some point in the day.

"I'm beginning to think my motivational words don't inspire him," Deepika told Juanita, after tossing the letter onto the bed in resignation.

"You have to keep saying them, Dee. Whether or not he admits it, he hears you, and they have an impact. You could say nothing and leave him to whither away completely alone, or you can say that you're there and that you believe in him. His parents were never there for him, you told me that yourself. Sometimes all anyone needs is for a person to tell them they care."

"Okay, so I say that I care. But I am here in the middle of France studying what I love in the stunning Côte d'Azur with my best friend and my boyfriend, and my father is alone in a prison of sorts while I eat freshly baked croissants and visit local boulangeries each morning, sip on fine Chardonnay in the evenings, something *he* introduced me to yet can no longer drink, and walk the beautifully-lit streets at nights with the man I love. That's what I'm doing. Do you still think I care enough?" Deepika concluded her rant and tried to catch her breath as the overwhelming emotion began to release its grip on her throat.

Juanita knew her friend so well. Of course this was how she'd react. She'd feel the guilt of a thousand nights, nights that she'd been out with her friends, busy studying, or enjoying herself, while her mother had been alone with her drunken father. She'd feel all that guilt, guilt that should belong not to her, but to her father. Her capacity for sensitivity and emotion had the potential of destroying her, but Juanita would not let that happen to her best friend. She wrapped one arm around Deepika's shoulder and said something that she knew would cheer her friend up not because it was tailored that way, but because it was genuine.

"Yes, you *are* in the French Riviera, eating baguettes, sipping fine wine, and exploring the coast…and French kissing your boyfriend on the beach…" Juanita added, playfully, in attempt to get a smile out of Deepika. It worked, but she also got a semi-expected slap on the shoulder!

Juanita laughed but then continued more seriously, "But do you know why you are here? Because you worked your ass off at school, managed to get a TA position in undergrad which is pretty much unheard of in the Lit department, and still make your professors wonder how on earth you are so damn smart in just your fourth year! And you know what? Do you really think your mother or father would want you to forgo this opportunity? Do you think they blame you for their own flaws because they don't, Deepika. And one more thing, since when do you have to pay for everyone's mistakes? You know, you've done this before with that boy back in high school. Don't do it with your family. They love you too much to watch you cry."

Deepika was in awe at Juanita's words. Her friend loved to use humour to lighten the mood, but when she said something

104

genuinely poignant, like she just had, it always left her speechless. She stood up and hugged her friend tightly, and then joked, "Better switch your major back to Philosophy, Cruz." They laughed together because Juanita had originally planned to do so until her passion for music overshadowed her interest in Philosophy. Although she would have loved to stay and join Deepika and William on their trek up the Nietzsche Path to see the village of Eze, she had band practice at their university, the Université Nice Sophia Antipolis, or UNS – apparently that was *le plus cool façon de dire la même chose* according to one of the boys who also played trumpet in the university's band. Just a few minutes after Juanita had grabbed her trumpet case and bolted out the door to get to the rehearsal hall, a ten-minute walk from residence, William was outside her door ready to hike.

"Have I told you how sexy you look in your athletic gear?" he smirked at Deepika, as they got into the bus that would take them to the bottom of the footpath.

Deepika laughed as she caught him staring at her ass, "Si tu fait trop d'attention à mon derrière, tu ne seras pas capable de me rattraper, Moreau!"

William couldn't control his laughter, so much so that the other people on the bus were either smiling or wondering what on earth could have been so *drôle* so as to have these two tourists in such a fit of laughter.

"We'll see who will have to catch up to who!" he laughed again before he kissed Deepika's cheek affectionately. William spent the rest of the one-hour bus ride reading one of his books from class, while Deepika wrote poetry in her travel-sized notebook she had brought with her to record lines that appeared in her mind without warning and then vanished within seconds if they were not written down. She flipped through a few full pages, some of which she had filled almost three years ago when she had been travelling, and caught sight of a couple lines that reminded her of how hard she had fallen for a boy she had considered one of her best friends. He hadn't been there to catch her, and that's when she had written the following lines, words that she would never forget: *Maybe you love him because there's something missing in you that he has. Maybe you love him because he loves himself.* That was something Juanita had criticized her for when she had been crying over her lost friend.

He had left her when she had done nothing but care for him. Juanita had said that something was lacking within her for her to be so distraught over that fool, and she needed to find out what that was. *No one can fulfill you but yourself, and deep down, you know that.*

"What are you thinking about?" William was looking at her now. He had stopped reading when he noticed that her pen had stopped moving in the corner of his eye. When she didn't start again for a while, he had to know what was on her beautiful mind. Deepika was caught off-guard by his question. Well, she was thinking about another man, but not in the way he would have taken it if she'd just said that, so she just shook her head and muttered that she couldn't think of what to write.

William chuckled and took one of her hands before whispering, "Write about that." He pointed out the window so they could both admire the Mediterranean coastline. The sea was the most dazzling hue of azure, and had the windows been down, Deepika was sure that she would be able to smell tropical paradise. The water was so mesmerizing that the bus had stopped at the bottom of the Nietzsche Path before they knew it. When they got off, they both gazed up the steep incline they were about to embark on, and then exchanged a knowing glance.

"Okay, let's just focus on the delicious crêpes and coffee we are going to have after this climb," William joked, sounding slightly nervous.

Deepika caught the hesitation in his voice and laughed, "Don't worry, I'll make sure you don't fall behind, Moreau."

With that, William bounded up the first few steps without waiting for Deepika, just to see her reaction. She knew he was being silly, so she began climbing the steps at a manageable pace and called out, "Keep that up, and you'll be fast asleep by the halfway point!"

He burst into a fit of laughter and waited for her to reach him. When she was just one step below, he held out his hand and smiled when she took it and rolled her eyes at him. They'd been walking in silence for twenty minutes or so, just taking in their surroundings, the brilliant green flora and the strikingly blue depths of the sea, when Deepika sighed thoughtfully and said, "There is no way I'd be able to do this, to be here with you, to be here at all, if my parents weren't the way they are."

William's attention had shifted to his girlfriend the second he had heard her sigh, and her comment made him smile because he had noticed that for the number of times she'd complained about her father, and sometimes her mother, there were a thousand more occasions upon which she would praise them both.

"And how are they?" he asked, wanting to know every detail about her.

"They support my dreams," Deepika smiled and continued after she squeezed William's hand, "And I know how crazy some of them are. I want to be a published author, I want to do trips like these to other places, learn more languages, and eventually, I want to teach Comparative Literature. I want all of that, and I know that's not the typical route people expect from me. They expect something in medicine, or something with more stability, but maybe I've never been a stable person."

William was stunned, and if he could have fallen deeper in love with this girl, if there were any more room for such a thing, it would have happened at that exact moment.

"You're a lucky girl to have parents like that. And hey, I know that despite all those wonderful things, parents can be a pain and won't understand every move you make, but want to know one thing I've learned in the past few years?"

Deepika was intrigued to know what he would say, especially because he was slightly older than her, so she nodded.

William smiled and finished his thought, "I used to think that I had to justify every single one of my moves – that if I didn't, then maybe I was doing the wrong thing. If I didn't have a list of calculated reasons for going through with something, I would be fearful because I would assume I was making a mistake. But, I'm 22 years old now, and I've had so many experiences, like coming to Toronto, meeting you, and now I'm here studying in France. I didn't have a list. I didn't go to every one of my relatives and explain to them why it was so important for me to do this. I knew what I wanted, and you don't always need to convince the world before going for it. Sometimes, all you need is to convince yourself and hope that your core support system will be there for you."

"Wow, I've just always felt the need to justify my every action, but you're right," Deepika thought, remembering how she would stress over pitching something to her parents, as if she were selling a product, and said, "People do usually know what they want. They're just afraid of others' reactions."

He couldn't have agreed more with her. They learned a lot about each other during the hour-long trek up to Eze, and when they finally reached the peak, they decided to sit on the outdoor deck at Chateau Eza, a 400-year old hotel in the middle of the village, to learn even more. There, they ordered the savoury crêpes they had been dreaming about at the bottom of the steps, and sipped steaming hot coffee while talking about their plans for the days to come.

With all the activities they had planned, Deepika had forgotten to call Jitendra that day, so her disheartened father had returned to his room at Bellwood feeling worse than he had when he had been told that his stay was to be extended.

Chapter 5

After a rough night, having heard nothing from Deepika and only getting half an hour with Asha, Jitendra had decided that he was going to be difficult today. He wasn't interested in breakfast or meditation, nor did he want to share his feelings at the group therapy session because his feelings consisted of a long incoherent string of curse words that he was sure would not be appreciated by anyone except John. After he had told John about the extension, the two of them joked about how it would be nice to rant about this crappy situation over whiskey. They had both agreed to sneak out of meditation so that they could chat in one of their rooms instead.

"I could use a cigarette," John sighed, as he plopped himself onto Jitendra's desk chair.

Jitendra laughed, although he did not smoke cigarettes, and added, "I just want to be on my patio at home, listening to Nina Simone, a cigar in my mouth, and a scotch in my hand…there's nothing much better than that."

The two new friends smiled at each other before John's voice of reason kicked in and he said, "Family. Family is better than that."

Jitendra had been thinking about that lately, and while he agreed, he also didn't think they needed him as much as everyone seemed to believe. His daughter had been too busy to call him. She had her own life now, and he didn't blame her for that. If he had been in her shoes, he would probably have taken a plane ticket to France as well. And now that she had her boyfriend, she had someone that Jitendra could tell would be there for her for a long time. It wasn't as though the two of them had a strong bond to begin with. With this guy in the picture, Jitendra felt as though he was completely out of the frame, especially when Asha told him that Deepika would call today and he had believed it, only to realize that she had become too preoccupied for him.

"Sometimes you need your family more than they need you, and sometimes you want them more than they want you," Jitendra said quietly, his mind wandering off to one of his favourite memories. He would never forget his wedding day, the day he had taken Asha Kaur as his wife. She was feisty, full of energy, and had as much of a sense of humour as he did…almost. He didn't think there could be any better match for him, so that day stuck in his mind like a story so touching one could never stop referring to it. It was his wedding that he always returned to whenever he had any kind of falling out with Asha. It was the one memory that made him think about what he could lose if he did not apologize to his wife or make the effort to sort out their differences.

"Jeet, are you ready yet?!" Gauri and Anita came running into the change room to see how their older brother was holding up. They were about to begin the ceremony, and everyone was waiting for the pandit to finish setting up.

"Wow, you are one lucky groom, and your wife-to-be is one lucky bride," Gauri smiled, as she squeezed her brother's shoulder. Jitendra was wearing a tan-coloured fitted wedding sherwani with deep red embroidery on it.

"Beta, Pandit Ji is ready to start," Jitendra's father, Dev Jha, entered the dressing room and didn't know what else to say other than gesture for his three children to take their seats. Jitendra had been hoping for some hint of genuine feeling in his father's eyes or a word of encouragement or two, but he received nothing of the sort, as usual. His youngest sister could sense what he was feeling and whispered that he looked very handsome and would do great. With that, Jitendra held his head up and went to sit under the ceremonial tent next to his veiled bride. The pandit began chanting in some ancient language that neither Jitendra nor Asha could understand. At one point, Jitendra was so bored with the proceedings, that he nudged Asha playfully to see if she would laugh. She chuckled softly, but glared at him through the flowery veil warning him not to laugh during the ceremony because it was disrespectful. Jitendra understood that, but he knew that most of the stuff the pandit spewed was religious, and he was not one for religion. Still, he had to please the family and sit through the incomprehensible babblings of this overweight man whose bare stomach was collecting beads of sweat because it was so close to the fire. Jitendra glanced at Asha and could see that she was probably thinking the exact same thing because the second she felt his eyes on her, she lifted hers from the pandit's oozing stomach and suppressed a laugh.

Jitendra couldn't keep himself from laughing in the dorm room as he remembered the funny moment between him and Asha at their wedding. John didn't even ask what was so funny, but rather, he started cackling like a madman when he heard Barbara shouting down the hallway asking if anyone had seen Jitendra Jha and John Milow. Hearing her panicked voice made Jitendra laugh even louder as well. Perhaps they were mad men. Two mad men trapped in a place neither of them really wanted to be. One of them had a guilty conscience, and the other had nothing else to go back to.

After being reprimanded by not only Barbara but also by one of her assistants, Jitendra and John both returned to their rooms. The entire time he was being disciplined, he maintained his composure because he had made up his mind. Nothing they told him was going to help at that point. Come tomorrow morning, he was a free man. He was done with rehab, and the only thing he felt that he had gotten out of it, was a temporary friend who understood him. None of this mattered. The next morning, he was up at 6 A.M. with everything packed. He told the receptionist at the front desk that he was checking out for good. He had written a brief note to Barbara, thanking her for her efforts and telling her that they were not entirely in vain, that he had learned more about himself in this place than he would have if he had never joined. Maybe it wasn't what Barbara or Asha would have hoped that he had learned, but sometimes outcomes are unexpected. With that, he left the centre and took a taxi to his office. He stayed there for a while, browsing the Internet, catching up on news, and checking his Facebook account to see how his daughter was doing. She had posted pictures with her boyfriend, and Jitendra couldn't help but smile when he saw how happy she looked with him. Perhaps he was what she needed, he thought. Perhaps he would be the man in her life who wouldn't hurt her.

Jitendra had fallen asleep at his desk when his cell phone rang. He glanced confusedly at the clock. 6 P.M. It was a Saturday, so who could be calling him at this hour? Thinking it could be Deepika, although she wouldn't expect him to have his phone on him, he grabbed the phone hurriedly anyway only to hear an automated machine on the other end asking him if he would like to partake in a survey on duct cleaning services. *How many duct cleaning services would I know about,* he rolled his eyes as he slammed the phone back onto the receiver. He could use some whiskey right about now, he thought. The closest LCBO was right around the corner by Fairview Mall. He didn't waste a minute to think about the consequences of doing what he craved. He didn't have much impulse control – the lack of reasoning was what led him into so much trouble so frequently, whether it was with his wife, daughter, or more recently, the police. He didn't care anymore. He was done with trying to please everyone around him when he had decided that he didn't want to be saved. A couple of hours later, he was back in his office, halfway through a bottle of Chivas with a pen in his hand and a piece of blank paper between his fist and the desk. He was about to start writing a letter for his daughter. He wasn't sure why he was doing so, but something beyond his control told him that he needed to do this. He wanted to give her something special for her graduation. He hadn't bothered to dilute his alcohol nor use a glass. He tilted the medium-sized bottle to his lips and took a shot of whiskey every few minutes. It pushed him to be as raw and emotional as he had ever been in any communication with his family. *Maybe if my parents had been more open, more communicative with me, maybe I would have been a stronger father to you,* he thought as he began to write to Deepika.

He spent a couple of sentences apologizing for his mistakes, but for the most part, he did not want her to pity him. He wanted her to take every good thing he had ever given her and apply it in the future. He wanted her to be that confident young woman that she was growing into – the woman that would steal everyone's attention, not because she was beautiful, but because she was intelligent and captivating whenever she spoke. He didn't want her to fear the possibility that she could become him. He wanted her to know exactly who he was, inside and out, and then to decide which parts of him she valued enough to emulate and which parts of him she despised, so that she would never look for those qualities in a partner. He didn't want her to feel as though it was her duty to save him, or any man that walked into her life. *You should never be with someone because you feel like you need to save them or fix them,* he remembered Asha saying something similar to Deepika after Deepika had had her heart broken by one of her friends. He wasn't the best at talking about those sorts of things, but he could see that Deepika had grown after that experience. She was more careful, but still the caring girl that would run to her friends if they needed help even if she knew that they would never reciprocate. She was that girl who would not lessen her generosity or her love just because she

112

didn't get the same amount in return. After all, she had loved him, a father who did not know how to display the same kind of affection. Finally, he could see a man that was returning her love, and he was happy that her daughter was getting the care she had deserved. He smiled and sealed the envelope with shaking hands. He left the letter on his desk, turned up his personal radio to his favourite jazz station, and leaned back in his chair as he enjoyed the alcohol he had left. This was his happy place. With the music on, the drugs in his system, his mind did not dare go to those dark places he feared the most. This was his happy place.

Chapter 6

Asha bolted through the double doors of Bellwood Health Centre, hardly taking a second to catch her breath, before she shouted at the receptionist, "Where's my husband?!" She was frantic, her hair done-up in a messy ponytail, as her eyes darted from the receptionist to the hallway down which she saw an anxious-looking Barbara striding towards her.

The receptionist didn't need to ask Asha for her name to know that she was referring to Jitendra Jha, the witty, smart-ass, yet horribly non-cooperative patient who had checked out early yesterday morning without any notice to inform his family of his whereabouts. In fact, the receptionist recalled his careless, nonchalant demeanour as he walked out of the building with his suitcase and a brief acknowledgement for Barbara that he had asked her to pass on, which she did immediately upon his leaving. She had paged Barbara right away, informing her that Mr. Jha had quit the program and hadn't left any instructions for them to contact his family. Given that he was an adult, the centre's staff had no obligation to phone anyone regarding his leaving, but Barbara had a soft spot for Jitendra despite him being so difficult. She couldn't help but feel a pang of sadness that he had not said goodbye to her before leaving. Perhaps she could have convinced him to stay. After the momentary hurt, she had remembered her professional self and had decided that she would call Asha Kaur to let her know what had happened. Something had told her that Jitendra had no immediate plans of returning home. After everything he had divulged about his family, she could not imagine him willingly going to face a deeply disappointed wife, and most of all, she could not see him calling his daughter and ruining her trip with the news. Concern for her former patient's mental state, a genuine sympathy for the man, and an inherent longing to always help others, whether they were strangers or friends, had driven the Admissions Counsellor to pick up the phone and ask Asha to come in for a meeting so that they could talk about Jitendra's sudden leave.

Now Mr. Jha's terrified-looking wife stood in front of her, with tears in her eyes threatening to fall at any second, and Barbara lost all sense of professional duty out of pure sympathy. She wrapped the woman she hardly knew in a tight hug and led her to her office where they could talk. She watched Asha's pained expression turn more pronounced when she told her that Jitendra had left yesterday morning without a word of where he was going, without any indication of regret or pain in his tone or expression.

"To tell you the truth, I am worried about his mental state," Barbara spoke solemnly, her voice softer than ever, before she added, "Do you have any idea where he might be?"

Asha couldn't suppress her tears any longer because the worst possibility had entered her already fragile mind, and she was so troubled that her instinct could be right, that she couldn't find the words to answer Barbara's question. She finally gathered the strength to look back at the kind eyes watching her concernedly and whisper, "A friend's place, maybe, or…"

Asha didn't really think that he had gone to a friend's place because she was sure that friend or that friend's wife, rather, would have called her as soon as he stepped into their home, likely without his consent. The fact that that hadn't happened yet made her fear the state he could be in. *Tired, alone, lost, inebriated, hurt, in pain…dead?* Her heart almost stopped at the last possibility, but she could not deny that it was a real prospect. She believed this because she had seen her husband in his darkest place. The night his best friend had died, she had found him in their garage with a bottle of whiskey. He had been sitting by the front tire of the car with the keys in his hand, twirling the key chain around his index finger as he sat there looking exhausted from all the crying, with his eyes glazed over and his mind somewhere else. She had taken a couple of minutes to process the sight before she'd run down the steps and grabbed the keys from him the second he'd stood up to get into the car. It had taken her a while before she had realized what he had intended, but the instant it had clicked, she had sped over to his side and had hugged him desperately, begging him to come inside the house and reminding him of everything he would lose should he choose to suffocate in that garage, alone.

Asha shuddered at the memory, but she couldn't help but think what may have happened had she not needed to get the chicken from the outside freezer to thaw for dinner. She would have assumed that he was upstairs in the attic watching TV, or reading a book in their room. He would leave lights on everywhere, so it was always difficult for her to know where he was in the house if he was not with her. The more Asha thought about it, the more she couldn't shake the dreadful feeling building in her stomach, turning her insides black, ready to consume her until there was nothing left but a pile of ashes. Was anyone there to save him this time, she thought. Who would pull him back from the edge if he was alone? He had too many unhappy memories for him to latch onto something positive of his own accord. Staying at that the rehab facility was pointless, so Asha decided it would be better for her to go home and call Jeet's friends to see if they had spotted him anywhere. She began to get up when the receptionist entered Barbara's office wearing a combination of a horrified and deeply distressed expression. Before Barbara could ask what the matter was, a female police officer stepped into the office and was about to ask for Jitendra Jha's counsellor when she caught sight of Asha Kaur looking devastated. The officer pursed her lips, and her sombre expression told everyone in the room what they couldn't bear to hear.

"I am so sorry, Mrs. Kaur," the officer used that gentle tone she must have had many occasions to practice because it was so calm and calculated that Asha broke. She slumped back into the seat she had gotten up from two minutes ago, with streaks of hot water coating her cheeks, yet she hardly made a sound. She did not get up and scream or throw things. She didn't shout at the ceiling, demanding how on earth Jeet could do this to her. She didn't say a word, and her muffled sobs were the only sound in the room for a while as she fell limp in the chair with her head in her hands and her heart in her throat.

Barbara's own heart broke when she saw the crumbling woman before her – a woman who had a brilliant daughter and had just lost her beloved husband who had been unable to compensate for what had been lacking within him. The counsellor could say nothing comforting at this time despite having gone through rigorous training and having years of experience dealing with aggrieved people. This was a special case. Jitendra Jha had been a special case she had been unable to crack, and now, telling his wife that everything would be okay, something she had said on countless occasions, seemed utterly preposterous and inappropriate not because it wasn't true, but because it was not enough. It was just not enough for this special case. All she could do was gesture for her colleague to speak with the officer while she offered physical warmth to Asha by wrapping a blanket around her and offering her a hand to hold while she took in what had occurred. Asha's mind was no longer in that suffocating room. Her hand was being held by this soft-spoken, sympathetic stranger, but she didn't feel that either. Her eyes had fixated on a little ornament that she had seen when she'd first entered the room. It was on the edge of Barbara's desk. It was of a couple that was slow dancing together, and it twirled automatically without a sound. Her eyes fixated on it and she drifted away under some kind of hypnosis.

They were married. The pandit had finished his unintelligible chanting hours ago, and now they were just finishing the speeches.

"No more talking," Jeet sighed as he kissed his bride's cheek, "I just want to dance already!"

Asha laughed at his comment and said, "Come on, Jeet. Your friends put in a lot of thought for these speeches, at least let them finish!"

He smiled, but mumbled, "Speeches are overrated." He had some alcoholic concoction in his hand that Asha thought must have been the cause of both his impatience and cheeriness. She hadn't known that he was a fan of dancing. They'd never done it together, not that they had been seeing each other for long before they'd decided to tie the knot, but still, this sudden eagerness Jeet had to dance took her by surprise. She knew that he adored music. He had introduced her to so many artists over the span of just a few days, but her favourites were all from the 80s. *What crap,* he had laughed when she'd admitted that to him the third time they'd gone out for a meal. *You should be listening to more Zeppelin and AC/DC and less ABBA*, he had teased. She laughed out loud, causing him to glance at her wondering what on earth he had missed in the awfully boring speech his cousin was in the midst of giving. She just shook her head and whispered that it was almost over.

"Cheers to that," Jitendra smiled and downed the rest of his drink. Asha shook her head, half-entertained, and half-disapproving. She wasn't very fond of drinking. She would drink on occasion, but it was hardly ever a thought that came to her on its own. Either a friend would suggest it, or Jitendra would offer to get her a glass. She pushed her displeasure to the back of her mind when her tipsy husband offered her his hand and tilted his head towards the dance floor just as the upbeat bhangra music began to play. A smile that reached her eyes splayed across her face and she shook her head at her inability to resist the handsome man who was grinning at her, a man who had chosen her, as she forwent all initial hesitation and unabashedly placed her hand in his. It was that night that she learned that Jitendra Jha had no clue how to dance. She giggled at his movements, but she could see the fire in his eyes, the way he felt the music rush through his bones. The real effect it had on him was not lost on her. He wasn't a good dancer by any means, but he was a passionate one. The enjoyment on his face, intensified by his lack of inhibition, the way he pulled her close and twirled her around the room, and the way he would try to sing along but mess up the lyrics because his Punjabi had faded after all his years growing up in Canada made her fall in love with him even more because even though she knew that he was three quarters of the way to being completely drunk, this was real.

Asha snapped out of her trance when Barbara finally gathered the courage to speak to her.

"Mrs. Kaur?" she asked, hesitant to say much else.

Asha glanced up, certain that her eyes were red and puffy from all the crying, and then spoke, her voice struggling to be heard, "I need to speak to the police officer."

"Of course, of course," Barbara stood up and invited the officer in.

Asha could see that the officer had a permanent look of compassion plastered on her face, and she couldn't help but wonder how many times a week this officer had to knock on doors of unsuspecting families, interrupting their children's games of hide-and-seek, silencing the music being played through the halls, shattering glasses that were being held casually seconds before hearing gut-wrenching news.

The officer introduced herself, but Asha couldn't even remember her name by the end of it. All she heard were the words *alcohol poisoning*, playing on a loop in her head. Nothing that was said after that was absorbed because the thoughts in her mind had been spiralling out of control, inching her closer to madness. She could not believe that this was happening again. She saw herself in a morgue. The medical attendant lifted the sheet, and she saw her father. Kartik Kaur. Time of death: Unknown. Cause of death: Car crash due to inebriation. She shut her eyes tightly and imagined herself in a morgue again, but this time, a different one.

This time she was in Toronto without her mother. This time she lifted the sheet without the help of the medical examiner to reveal a pale, blue-tinged face that she had been used to seeing flushed red. Jitendra Jha. Time of death: Approximately 2:30 AM on Monday October 28, 2016. Cause of death: Pulmonary aspiration and significant dehydration. Asha opened her eyes with a start, not wanting to see those pictures any longer, and stood up from her seat calmly. She thanked the officer for her offer to provide a police escort to the hospital and said that she needed to call her daughter before she could see her deceased husband.

As she walked to her car, she saw something new in that white Range Rover that she had previously despised. It was *his* car. In that moment, she saw him in the driver's seat drumming his fingers on the steering wheel as he swayed to the saxophone solo he was listening to. She saw Deepika roll her eyes in the backseat when her father started to sing, and she saw herself applying her lipstick in the passenger seat as they drove to a friend's house together. She approached the front door, opened it slowly, and sat in the seat for a while. She saw the faded coffee stains left by Jeet's daily Americano Mistos from Starbucks by the gearshift that she had been meaning to wipe away for weeks and smiled. She opened the glove box and found Jeet's favourite lighter, some old packs of gum, and his iPod classic. Taking a deep breath, she shut the compartment, and turned the ignition on. This was the first time in a while that she had driven without any music in the background. Her head was too crowded with ideas on how she would tell Deepika what had happened. It was almost 3 P.M. in Toronto, which meant that it was about 9 P.M. in France, she calculated mentally. How could she break such awful news to her daughter, when she was certain her daughter was out with her friends at this hour having fun? She knew her daughter well, and she knew that if she kept her husband's death from Deepika even a day longer than she should, Deepika would be even more devastated. Asha hated the thought of destroying her daughter's trip, but she needed her daughter at this time, and her daughter had to come home.

It was almost funny that after being hit with the worst news imaginable, one was expected to set aside one's own grief for a few days to make phone calls and funeral preparations, to clean out the deceased's office, to call credit card companies and banks, to notify anyone else who could be affected by the person's death because that was the responsible thing to do. How absurd it was to expect a person who had the ground pulled from underneath them in a matter of hours to treat her situation as a fact of life and move on just enough so that the rest of the world could too, Asha thought.

Upon reaching her house, she walked inside feeling absolutely dejected. She shoved her depression to the back of her mind, as she was expected to, and made her way to the kitchen table to sit by the phone. She wasn't prepared to make this call by any means. The only consolation she had was the fact that her daughter wasn't alone because had that been the case, there would be no way Asha would have been able to go through with this. Everyone was wrong when they said that there was nothing more painful and more difficult than childbirth because the thought of relaying Jeet's death over the phone to her daughter ripped her to shreds. She pinched the bridge of her nose with her fingers anxiously, unable to cry anymore as her tear ducts were completely dry. No amount of deliberation or rehearsal could prepare her for this, but it had to be done.

Chapter 7

"I can't believe I didn't even call him," Deepika stated listlessly, her eyes focused on the white wall in front of her.

She struggled to keep them open. She hadn't slept a wink last night after her mother had called. She had been in shock, unable to process the words, asking over and over if she had heard correctly, if this was some cruel joke, if the woman on the other end had the wrong number and this was a different Jitendra. After the shock, she had cried all night. She had told Juanita to get some sleep, but she had been unable to get rid of her boyfriend. William had stayed awake with her and held her, refusing to leave even when she'd told him that she'd be all right. She didn't want him to lose sleep over this. *Don't be ridiculous,* he had said, and then shut the door and climbed into bed with her to hold her as she wept for her father.

"How could I forget to call him?" Deepika said again, her eyes moistening for the umpteenth time. William could see that she was about to blame herself for her father's death but wouldn't allow it. Before he could interject, she began, "What if all he needed was a call from me? What if that's all he needed to stay?"

He had been hearing Deepika's self-loathing for hours, and it tore him apart. It broke his heart to see her in so much pain, but it just destroyed him to hear her actually think that her father had given up on everything because she hadn't called.

"Dee," William said softly, pulling her into his arms at the same time, "You can't blame yourself for your father's actions. He was an unhappy man, Deepika. You did everything you could to try to heal whatever brokenness was inside him, but remember what you told me? Only you can fulfill yourself. It had to come from within. It's not your fault – I can't take you hurting yourself like that when it's not true."

Deepika was quiet aside from her consistent sobbing. She couldn't stop no matter how hard she tried. It all hurt too much. Every single occasion on which she had cursed her father came rushing back and hit her with brute force, each time she had told him she hated him flooded her head and ricocheted off all sides of her brain with no signs of stopping, and it felt as though any happy memory they had shared had been erased from existence.

"Hey," William rubbed Deepika's shoulder gently when she had stopped crying, likely because she too, had run out of tears. He continued sweetly, "Come on, you haven't eaten in so long. Let me order something for the three of us, okay? Juanita should be here soon. She's booked us flights back for tonight."

Deepika wasn't registering a word William was saying until she heard him mention the flights. Plural. She snapped out of the trance she was in in a flash and grabbed his hand, the one that was resting on her knee.

"Don't you dare screw up your trip for me, Moreau," she was serious as she spoke, and then she added, "And what the hell is Juanita thinking? Absolutely not. She's wanted to study in this music program for years! We talked about it back in high school."

William placed his other hand over Deepika's and smiled, "I'm coming back with you, Dee. The only reason I came was because of you. I've seen this place twice before. It's not nearly as precious as you and your family."

Deepika sighed, hating the feeling that because William and Juanita loved her so much, they were actually willing to forgo their trips. William she could understand a bit more because he did mainly come so that he could take a trip with her, but Juanita? There was no way in hell she would let her best friend miss this opportunity. So when Juanita walked into the room solemnly with the pizza that William had ordered for the three of them just half an hour later, Deepika demanded that she cancel her flight back. They argued back and forth for another thirty minutes until Juanita finally gave in and cancelled her ticket. *I will never speak to you again if you miss out on your dream for me. I know you're here for me, Cruz.* That was what made Juanita stop fighting with her friend and cancel the ticket on her laptop in front of Deepika so that she would believe that it was actually done.

A few hours later, Deepika called her mother to let her know that she and William were about to board the plane and would take a cab back to the house so she didn't need to worry about picking them up. Asha didn't know what to say, but she felt terrible about all of this, so she apologized as if it were her fault that her husband had drunk himself to death, as if she had been the one to force the alcohol down his throat in such a brief period of time, as if she had been the one to find him slumped in his office chair with his torso

123

sprawled across his desk and his head resting in the bit of vomit that he'd managed not to choke on. Asha had been relieved that she hadn't been the one to enter his office to find him that way because just the thought of seeing his lifeless body in such an undignified state made her feel like retching. It had been an employee who had found him and called 911 without a moment's hesitation. Asha knew David from the couple of instances that Jitendra had invited him over for cocktails after work and had spoken to him over the phone to make sure that he was okay – after all, who could bear such a sight and be totally unaffected? The man was so young, just in his late 20s, and for him to be thrown into a distressing situation like this made Asha's heartache. She could hardly imagine finding Jitendra that way, and she was nearing 50 years of age. The poor boy, who had simply been looking for IT experience to pad his resume, had been embroiled in a plot so dismal and unendurable for those involved that Asha had called him to her home for a meal that same evening before Deepika and William were to return. Even though her heart, mind, and body had suffered an egregious amount in such a short period of time, she felt guilty and wanted to make sure the young man, young enough to be her son, was going to be okay. When Asha revealed this to Deepika over the phone, her words were met with an audible gasp, followed by a silence that felt like hours, and finally, a broken *that's awful* probably to put an end to the quiet between them than anything else.

There was nothing left to say, so Asha wished her daughter a safe flight and hung up the phone all while thinking what a mess this was. What a horrifying, unprecedented, unfathomable mess. She thought about the last time she had visited Jitendra and couldn't believe how quickly things had changed. He had been in a cheery mood when she'd seen him last – all smiles and no complaints – and he had promised her that he'd been making progress and was happy to have enrolled. He would have known that Barbara could not disclose the reality to her out of confidentiality, Asha thought. He would have known that and would have said everything possible to keep her at peace. She should have known better, she scolded herself. She should have been stronger than to have accepted his words and been taken in by his charm and forged smile just because it had been convenient and preferable to believe that. It was all too familiar. When her father had died, she had had so much faith in his words. He had told her that he'd try harder and she had trusted him. How foolish was she to have made the same mistake twice? The men in her life had let her down so many times, anyone else would have given up hope entirely. Was she crazy for thinking things would be different every time, or did she value people so much because she saw their individuality and refused to group them all into the same category? She pondered the question but came up with up nothing. And then something hit her. She was wrong. Not all the men in her life had let her down. Not her daughter's boyfriend. He had taken such great care of her daughter that she could not imagine that ceasing any time soon. Not her uncle and aunt, Raj and Anjali, who had been her second set of parents, especially after her father had died. Not her father's colleague and wonderful friend, Rahul, who had stepped in as a surrogate paternal figure the minute he had seen her break at her father's lifeless body on the morgue table. What she was thinking right now, to be able to see the light in the midst of darkness, that was her greatest strength. It was awfully difficult to ignore an indistinguishable glow of positivity when it emanated from her spirit and refused to remain locked up.

A few hours later, Deepika and William had arrived in Toronto and were helping with funeral preparations. Jitendra's parents were supposed to fly in around 1:30 AM, and they had refused to take a taxi back to the house, as Asha had predicted, so William offered to pick them up with Deepika. Asha was astounded at the young man's initiative. He was a gentleman through and through – that, she did not deny – but this was something she could not let him do.

"That's very sweet of you, William," Asha began, smiling at his generosity, "But it's way too late for you to be driving, and to pick up my parents-in-law, too!"

William laughed and looked at Deepika, who was now smiling for the first time in hours. A giggle escaped her as she remembered how late they'd stayed up in France and the number of times William had borrowed his relatives' car to take her and Juanita around the city.

"It's really no problem," he said finally, "In fact, I wouldn't mind going alone so you two can get some sleep, but to spare your parents an extreme amount of discomfort, I figure it would be best to go with Deepika."

Deepika laughed at his comment because it wasn't an exaggeration at all. Her grandparents would likely go into cardiac arrest if they were met by a French-speaking Caucasian man at the airport. *And let's face it, one funeral is enough*, Deepika thought. Her internal monologue surprised her because it almost made her laugh out loud. *Is this what it's like to be in shock?* She figured all the existentialist texts she'd read had rubbed off on her, and that the sudden burst of dark humour was inevitable. William was happy to see that Deepika was finally smiling even if it lasted just a minute and that Asha agreed to let him drive to the airport. She was too exhausted to argue with her daughter and her daughter's boyfriend on top of that, so she let them go a few hours later but made Deepika promise to text her when they reached and when they were heading back to the house.

She hated the thought of either of them leaving the house and driving so late at night, and she quietly cursed her in-laws for refusing to take a taxi back. They weren't the only ones to lose a loved one. Far from it. And yet, when Dev Jha had called the house, he had made a brief statement that they would need to be picked up, followed by the flight number. No condolences, no hint of emotion, nothing. Asha knew she had been foolish to expect her father-in-law to open up, or to offer some sense of paternal support considering she had lost her husband. She had done more for Jitendra in the twenty odd years they had been married than his parents had done for him in his lifetime, yet she was aware that she'd never receive that acknowledgment from them and that deep down, they would always despise her for pushing him into rehab. They would always see that as the reason for his death. They wouldn't dare look further and see the nightmares they had caused their son, nor the neglect that he had carried with him for years and could never seem to shake. No, because if they admitted that they had been horrendous parents, even for a second, then they would have to accept a hand in his death. Asha sighed at the prospect of having to be hospitable and warm towards her in-laws in just a couple of hours. It never seemed to end, and she couldn't help but wonder how on earth her own mother had had the time to grieve, if any. She sunk deeper into her chair and shut her eyes, hoping to sleep even just for a few minutes.

Meanwhile, William and Deepika were sitting in the Range Rover on the highway en route to the airport. Asha had insisted that he drive it because the other car wouldn't be large enough for Dev and Archana's luggage.

"How are you doing?" William interrupted the silence and glanced at his girlfriend quickly before turning his attention back to the road.

Deepika was quiet, but he heard her even though her voice was barely a whisper, "I'll never be able to call him again."

William couldn't think of anything worth saying, so he turned the volume up to hear Eric Clapton's acoustic version of "Layla" playing from Jitendra's connected iPod Classic, and dropped his hand from the gearshift and opened his palm for her to hold if she wanted. She did, and then she smiled when she heard the familiar tune and asked, "You know how my dad got me into guitar?"

"How?" William responded, genuinely curious and glad that she was talking to him. Suffering in silence could be the most torturous experience people willingly subjected themselves to, and he sure as hell didn't want his love to do that to herself.

Her smile widened as she remembered how reluctant she had been to practice when she had first started guitar lessons. She'd stomped her feet and made a huge fuss, and her mother had shouted at her for behaving badly, but her father had not said a word during her tantrum. He had watched his daughter's bad behaviour and had decided that he would try another way of getting through to her.

"He showed me a video of Eric Clapton's solo guitar performance of this very song," she grinned, as she sang the last lyric, and then continued, "He made me sit and watch the whole thing, and after the first thirty seconds, I was so mesmerized by it that I was quiet for the next five minutes. After that, he just looked at me and said: *Dee, that could be you. It's your choice.* And that's all he had to say. After that, I would practice for at least six hours a week on top of my school work, and I tried to learn everything – the classical stuff, this classic rock, top 40 radio, I even tried song-writing out. But if he hadn't pushed me, from day one, if he hadn't been the one to encourage me to pick an instrument and learn it, I don't know if I ever would have."

William smiled and squeezed her hand, "Your father was a good man, and I see you and what a bright young woman you are, talented in so many ways – writing, music, listening and counselling

– and despite everything unacceptable he did, he helped shape you into the remarkable girl that you are."

Deepika's cheeks grew warm, partially because of William's compliments, but also because she felt that she hadn't given her father enough credit when he had been alive. There had been a disconnect between them that they had found impossible to overcome entirely, and she couldn't help but think, had they managed to move past that, would he still be around? She almost felt closer to him now than when he had been alive. Things had a strange way of working themselves out sometimes, and she didn't know whether to be thankful that she was realizing how much her father had done for her, including all the little things, which happened to be a lot bigger than she had originally thought, or to be sad that she hadn't realized all this years ago.

"You know what's funny," Deepika said after a brief break in the conversation, "He quit guitar as a teenager. He never actually told me that, though. It was as though he thought that telling me that would make him out to be a hypocrite in my eyes and maybe lead me to quit as well. I just found some old guitar music books one day and saw his name scribbled in the top right corner and realized maybe he thought I could do what he couldn't. Maybe he just wanted me to be better than him."

William nodded as he listened to Deepika speak, and then simply said, "You are. And he was proud of you. Don't forget that."

With that, he turned into the airport parking lot and switched off the ignition after finding a spot by the appropriate terminal doors.

"Ready?" he looked at Deepika when he heard the click of her seatbelt as she took it off.

It was one thing to see her grandparents alone, but now she'd have to introduce her boyfriend and hope that they didn't make any rude comments towards him or her mother because she wouldn't be able to take that. She was hoping that they were too fatigued and upset to talk much. She rolled her eyes and threw William an exaggerated grimace when he looked at her questioningly.

"Not a chance."

He chuckled softly and exited the driver's seat before meeting her on her side and shutting the door for her. He wrapped one arm around her waist and pulled her against him so swiftly that it took her by surprise. She stared into his chocolate brown eyes and was enchanted by his long lashes and trademark half-smile that he'd always have on for her. He was dressed up quite a bit for the airport, kind of like her father used to. Jitendra used to wear black designer jeans, a sleek black belt, a crisp white Italian-made shirt, and either a grey or black dinner jacket to top it off every time he travelled. He had to look sophisticated, he used to say. *We don't need riff raff at the airport.* Deepika shook her head smiling as she remembered how she would also dress up like a businesswoman whenever they had travelled together and wouldn't care whether the destination was a blistering hot Mexico as long as she looked as professional as her father. She now admired William's army green dress shirt tucked into a pair of navy blue jeans, finished with a black belt. He caught her head in his hands and kissed her deeply, urgently, as if she were about to slip through his fingers. She hadn't felt that kind of desperation from him since one of their first nights in France when she had comforted him about his ailing grandfather in Quebec.

When he stopped kissing her, he was still holding her against him, so she smiled waiting for him to say something or nothing at all. Whatever he wanted to say, it was written all over his face.

He finally spoke, whispering loud enough for her to catch the words, "Je t'aime."

Even though he did this all the time, it still made her blush when he casually switched to French, especially when he was being extra affectionate, despite being almost equally as well-versed in English. It was in those deeply emotional moments, that he would revert to French, his mother tongue. And when she felt that same overwhelming emotion, she could try her hardest to say *Je t'aime* but all that came out was *I love you.* William understood the difficulty. It was the same reason his affection was strongest in French. Deepika noticed that he hardly had an accent, but it came through every now and then, and it made her love him even more.

She grinned at him and replied, "Je sais." When he laughed at her answer, she winked at him and reached for his hand so that they could walk to the terminal. She knew he was waiting for her to say it back, but she was overcome by a sudden bout of mischief, so she waited until they reached the doors before she threw her arms around his neck, taking him completely off guard, and kissed him back with the same energy he had just moments ago.

"I love you too."

They both laughed at each other's craziness and made their way to the Arrivals area of the airport hand-in-hand. Deepika didn't know how she would have managed all this without him, but she thought, it was always difficult to imagine an absence, especially when that person had inserted himself into her life in such a way that she couldn't picture him anywhere else.

They made their way to the waiting area and ordered coffees and doughnuts while they watched the screens for the flight's status. Airports had always been so exciting to Deepika, because she'd either be off to some place tropical or there to pick up a loved one. This time, the whole process was dreary, but the one thing keeping her together as she watched smiling faces shuffle in and out of the shops was by her side, and she knew that she'd be fine.

Chapter 8

After an annoyingly unnecessary amount of back-and-forth between Asha and Dev the morning after they had arrived, the two of them finally came to an agreement about the funeral arrangements. It was set for the day after tomorrow at 3 P.M.. In a frazzle, Asha mass-emailed their family friends circle and Jitendra's employees. Dev and Archana were expecting their two daughters to fly in from India in the afternoon. They were going to take a cab to the house, thankfully. Asha had called the closest friends personally to explain what had happened, and a few of them had already come by the house earlier in the evening to offer their condolences and support. Scheduling the funeral and sending the emails was easy. Both tasks required little thought or emotional investment. She was putting off the most daunting task because she didn't feel mentally prepared to do it. She didn't know if she'd ever be prepared, but the landlord had called her twice already telling her to clean out Jitendra's office otherwise his stuff would be disposed of. William had gone to the office with Deepika that morning to disconnect all the tech, including the computers and printers, and load it into the car. Deepika hadn't wanted to enter Jitendra's private office, so she let William go inside to get the computers and propped the doors open so that he could transfer all of it into the trunk. Deepika had stared in disbelief at all the stuff William had salvaged from the office, not knowing what they would do with all of it. She figured they would keep some of it and try to sell the rest. Luckily for William, some of Jeet's employees including David came by the house to help him with the computer equipment. They stored it in the basement until Asha and Deepika decided what they would do with it.

Asha made the decision to visit her husband's office after she had greeted his sisters, Anita and Gauri, both of whom were visibly devastated. She felt terrible for them because she knew how much their older brother had meant to them. He was the one who had taken care of Anita especially when their parents had left them alone uncaringly. Out of compassion, she made them tea and heated up some of the Indian food her friends had brought over despite feeling dreadful herself, and when they asked where the family albums were located, she didn't hesitate to bring them out and let the women look at all the happiness Jitendra had experienced in Canada with his family. With that, she shut the front door behind her, breathed a deep sigh, and got into her own Volvo this time. Deepika had taken the Rover out for a drive because she needed some space. The house was suffocating her. Even William went downtown to take a break and spend some time studying in the Starbucks he and Deepika frequented. He had received a distressed phone call from his family just hours after he had come back from France notifying him that his grandfather was in critical condition. He had yet to tell Deepika about it because he knew it would break her if she found out that he had to leave for Quebec and wouldn't be there for the funeral. His flight to Quebec City had been booked, however, and he was to leave tomorrow. Sitting the Starbucks, he contemplated just how he would break the news to her. He shook his head in frustration. This is just what she needed – another man to leave her alone in a time of need.

They'd both requested some time off school due to the unexpected circumstances. Deepika hardly had time to go to the registrar in-person and explain what had happened, but she had managed to get two weeks off because of her stellar grades and the fact that they had a temporary replacement TA available for her since she was no longer in France. Asha was glad that the two of them took some time to be out of the house because it was painful to be surrounded by all the memories, and the two sisters' wailing was even more excruciating to hear. Jeet wouldn't have wanted them to cry. If he could've sent them some kind of signal, he would have, and he would've told them to uncork a bottle of fine French wine, turn on the sound system and play Nina Simone, and dance. He would've wanted them to keep living, the way he believed life should be lived. Without pain, without stressing over the future. With love, with music, with food and drink. Even though Asha knew what he would've wanted, she also knew that his ideals could be unrealistic. The grief needed to be dealt with, not shoved to the side until one day it came rushing out so rough and fast that her body couldn't bear it.

Asha hesitated at Jeet's office door, but eventually turned the handle and went inside. There were loose sheets strewn across the desk and a bunch of files stacked on top of the filing cabinet. The paintings on the wall looked as new as ever, but other than the few trinkets on his desk – a few golf tees in the corner and a can of unopened Coca Cola – there was nothing that incited overwhelming emotion in the room other than the room itself. She walked over to his black ergonomic chair and sat down. The room smelled of disinfectant spray with a hint of vomit from the cleaning the cops had done. She began to look in the drawers and didn't see anything personal until she came across what appeared to be a photograph. Upon closer inspection, she saw that Jeet had kept the photo of them at their wedding reception tucked away in his drawer, for rainy days she supposed. She hadn't realized that she'd begun to cry until a tear moistened the glossy surface of the picture. She wiped it away hastily and put the photograph in a cardboard box she had brought with her. She knew that she'd have to go through the filing cabinet in case there were any important documents related to insurance or banking that she'd have to take home, but that was something she'd worry about later.

There was just one more thing in the drawer that Asha was surprised by, and that was a CD Deepika had gifted to her father years ago. Asha remembered Deepika complaining to her that Jitendra never seemed to appreciate her gifts, so when she put the CD in Jeet's portable sound system and heard the acoustic guitar versions of his favourite songs that Deepika had learned especially for his 50th birthday, she was moved to tears for a second time. Deepika would have been so happy to know that her father listened to her CD at work. Being in that office was surprisingly cathartic for Asha because she had walked into the room thinking that she'd be filled with greater dread than she had been before entering, but she received a form of closure as she packed away the photograph, the CD, a few sweatshirts he had kept, and lastly, a small leather journal. Who would have thought that Jitendra Jha kept a journal? Asha had had no idea that he, too, was a writer at heart. When she flipped through the pages, she saw his torment rise from the dried blue ink and materialize into a dark haze in front of her eyes and then evaporate into nothingness.

He had written about almost every major fight they had had, the times Deepika had screamed at him, but mostly, every time that he had been sorry. He had apologized in that journal, and somehow, knowing that despite the disappointing way in which he would shake off every argument they'd have, none of that carelessness he had

133

shown was genuine. What he had written, on the other hand, was real. As she skimmed the words, she was distraught at the self-loathing he had felt on so many different occasions. *Was that the same self-loathing her father had felt when he'd lost his prestigious position at the Delhi hospital? Was this bitterness within what drove them both to fatal ends?* The parallels were too much for Asha to take, and the mere suggestion that Jitendra's actions had been intentional was agonizing. It was better not to dwell on that, she thought. She was ready to sift through the files when she caught sight of a piece of paper jutting out of one of Jeet's folders. Curiously, she pulled it out only to find that he had dated it October 28, the same night he had died, and addressed it to their daughter. Asha didn't know what to think, but she hugged the envelope to her heart and inhaled the scent of his strong Ralph Lauren cologne that lingered on the paper. That letter must have been the last thing he had touched aside from the alcohol. She put it safely in her folder and made a mental note to give it to Deepika, but not now. No, this was the last thing her father had left for her. She wanted to keep it for a special occasion.

Sifting through the legal documents was quick. Asha thought it would be best to pack up all the files and take them home and store them just in case. When she had finished at the office, she stood in the doorway and took another look around the room. She closed her eyes for a minute, opened them again, and could see him sitting in his chair, leaning back with his Bluetooth headset on, speaking with stubborn clients. He sounded patient but his hands were in the air and he was shaking his head and rolling his eyes. Asha smiled at the sight. He picked up his coffee and sipped it while he checked his emails and even opened up Facebook so that he could see what Deepika had been up to. He grinned at her posts but didn't acknowledge them, and then he returned to reading *The Economist*. Asha sighed and flipped the light switch, and suddenly it was dark and the room was empty. The chair was vacant, the portable sound system was not on the shelf, his desk was bare, and all that remained was the sound of Asha's staggered breath.

While Asha returned home, William had decided that he needed to speak with Deepika immediately. He invited her out for a drink at a restaurant by her house, telling her that he needed to speak to her about something serious and that they could both use the drink and the night out. When he had called her, his tone of voice suggested that it wasn't good news. Deepika didn't know how much more heartache she could take, so she hoped that she'd be able to handle whatever it was he was going to throw at her. They sat by candlelight, and as they observed the menus, William attempted to converse with her on unrelated topics. She could tell that he was deflecting, so she waited for their orders to be taken before she asked him to tell her what was really on his mind. A gasp escaped her lips when he told her that his grandfather wouldn't be around much longer, and when she saw his lip quiver for a split second before he regained his composure, she wanted to shove the table keeping them apart aside and take him in her arms. William looked at her expectantly, thinking she'd piece together the bad news and the fact that his entire family was in Quebec, but she just said that she was sorry and asked if there was anything she could do to help. He figured that she had too much on her mind to realize the implications of what he had just revealed to her, so he took her hand in his and intertwined their fingers together, and in the most sincere voice he said, "I am so sorry this is happening right now. I have to fly home tomorrow, Dee, and I would have told you sooner but I only had a day to process this information myself."

He watched her face fall, but he could see that she was trying to be strong, so he continued, "It hurts me that I won't be there for you at the funeral, but I promise that I will be back as soon as I can. And you know you can call me any day, any time."

It took Deepika some time to register everything he had said, but after she had shed a few tears out of shock that he was leaving for an indefinite amount of time, she squeezed his hand and told him that she was also there for him in this difficult time. They would be there for each other.

"Hey," William spoke in a low voice and smiled, "I'm just a province away."

Deepika couldn't suppress her smile. She took a sip of her drink and let out a crazy-sounding laugh. William joined in because he knew what she was thinking. How ridiculous was their situation? How absolutely unprecedented and absurd!

"If we stop laughing, we'll go mad," Deepika commented, reading his mind. They raised their glasses and cheered to their equally depressing situations, and Deepika thanked her boyfriend for taking her out of that dark, abysmal house she was confined to for the majority of the day. She didn't know how to laugh in that house. Being there drained her of all her energy, made her lose sleep, and had her crying for hours for the man she had tried so hard to understand but could never get through to entirely. She knew that there was nothing she could do about it now, so she focused on enjoying her last night with William for what she envisioned would be quite a while. They were quiet as they ate their meals, but after a while, Deepika spoke up.

"I need you," she said, her voice was barely a whisper. She called the waitress over for the bill, while William was still trying to decipher what she'd meant.

"I'm here, baby, I always will be," he smiled, stroking her hand across the table, hoping he had understood her. He was confused. He'd never given her any reason to believe that he wouldn't be there for her.

Deepika smiled back at him, but there was desire surging through her. She'd had a couple of drinks, was mentally exhausted, and her gorgeous sensitive boyfriend was about to leave her for an indefinite amount of time the next day. She was a young woman. Couldn't he put together what she'd meant? She chuckled to herself as she paid for their meals, a bewildered William watching her after she'd refused to split. After saying thank you to the waitress, she got up and grabbed her boyfriend's hand.

"Is everything okay, Deepika?" he asked affectionately, as he followed her outside. Her current mood had taken him off-guard. She couldn't have meant what he was thinking, could she? He asked again, "What's the matter?"

Deepika couldn't control herself any longer, so she threw herself against him and crushed her lips against his in the middle of the parking lot, not giving a damn who saw, whether they were children or elderly people.

William chuckled against her lips and mumbled, "Oh, now I understand you."

Deepika laughed, texted her mother that she'd be home in the morning, and told William to drive them to his place. If he was going to leave her the next day, and if she wasn't going to know when he'd be back, then they were going to make the most of this night. She was done crying for today. She was done thinking. All she'd been doing is reflecting, and her head was going to explode if she ran any more alternate scenarios through it. They reached his place in no time, and she had him on the edge of his bed grinning like a handsome fool in seconds. She straddled him and whispered, "Je te veux maintenant." *I want you now.* She kissed down his jawline and up and down his neck before she said, "Take my mind off all this. I can't do it anymore."

William looked at her understandingly and tucked a strand of hair behind her ear. He wiped away a solitary tear that fell from his beautiful girlfriend's eye, telling her not to cry tonight, and simply said, "I'm yours tonight, tomorrow, forever until you no longer want me," before he lay her down and started making love to her so that the both of them could forget the crap they were going through right now. Before he could turn off the lights, she whispered lovingly, "Don't you know, I'll never stop wanting you, you idiot?" They both laughed, and Deepika closed her eyes in gratitude that she had him. She didn't know how else she'd make it through this tough time. He was just incredible. They spent the night in each other's arms offering physical comfort to one another. Enough talking had been done. Sometimes all you need is a kiss, a touch, a hug, to know that everything would be okay, Deepika thought. She turned into her boyfriend's arms and hugged him tightly, refusing to think about what might await her in the morning. Tonight she could be a 21-year old girl in love with a boy.

When Asha returned to the house, she found her mother-in-law standing by the stove and preparing fresh chicken biryani. It would take a few days before she'd get used to the fact that she had a full house considering she had been alone for nearly a month.

"Fresh chai banaa diya," Archana turned to look at Asha and gestured to the counter. Her voice took Asha by surprise, but the fact that she had made her a steaming hot cup of tea on top of being in the process of cooking dinner for all of them, that really impressed Asha.

"Thank you, Mum," she replied, sitting down at the kitchen table to drink it.

What followed was an exchange that neither of them had expected. Asha didn't think Archana Jha had a single maternal bone in her body, but she had tried. She'd told Asha that she was there for her and Deepika, that she thought the boy Deepika was with was very sweet and kind, that she was sorry for Dev's obnoxious behaviour upon arriving at the house, and that she hoped they could try to get along in the next couple of months because the tragedy of Jitendra's death had shocked everyone to the core. Asha agreed with her by the time the conversation ended and hoped that this wasn't just talk but a genuine desire to improve their relationship. It was time that they put their differences aside and remember what matters most was the fact that they all loved Jitendra. Perhaps Archana and Dev were terrible parents, but they loved their son. They just hadn't known how to display that affection and care. And while it was too late to learn, it wasn't too late for Asha to forgive them for neglecting their son and playing a huge part in contributing to his flawed character.

Deep down, Asha believed that she had been meant for Jeet. She'd married him to teach him lessons, but also to learn from him; he'd brought challenges to her life but also a lot of love, and a lot of fun; he'd helped build her into someone who could say that she was as strong as her mother had been; and finally, he'd given her the most loveable, brilliant, and affectionate daughter any parent could ask for. Of course, Asha was in pain at this loss, but she couldn't deny what she had gained from having had Jeet in her life for thirty some years – the most turbulent, enjoyable, and crucial years of her life. She and Deepika reflected on Jitendra's core qualities at the funeral the next day, remembering not to paint him as a perfect man, but as the flawed, yet genuine man they loved. Asha was relieved when her mother flew in from India that same night and told her that she'd stay with them for an extended period of time. Deepika was also thrilled to have her maternal grandmother at home.

They went to the funeral together. It was at a funeral home just twenty minutes from their home. Deepika was overwhelmed by the number of people that had shown up, many of whom she hadn't met before, but she watched as they struggled to wipe their moist eyes from under their sunglasses. It was tough for her to be there. It hadn't truly felt real until she saw the closed pearly white casket at the front of the room, and as much as she'd love to see his face one more time, he'd never wanted a viewing. She'd placed pictures of him around the casket, with his friends, his family, but the most precious one to her was this photo of the two of them when she was just ten years old. She'd just begun to learn the guitar and he was kneeling in front of her, helping her place her fingers on the appropriate strings. Deepika took her sunglasses off and slipped them into the front of her shirt. She picked up the picture frame and gave her tight throat some relief by allowing herself to bawl. A few of her father's friends looked concerned but they didn't have the guts to comfort her. She didn't want them to anyhow. They were just Jitendra's friends. They weren't his daughter. They hadn't lived with him. They couldn't love him the way she did. She hugged the photograph to her chest and tried to calm down, but anxiety washed over her and she couldn't seem to slow her breathing. Suddenly, she felt someone's hand on her back and turned in surprise, only to find her mother's favourite aunt and uncle standing there with sympathetic looks.

"Raj Uncle?" she asked, a hint of uncertainty in her voice. She'd only met Raj and Anjali once in her life and she'd been relatively young, but she'd seen them in photos and remembered the descriptions her mother would provide whenever she was sharing stories of her childhood.

"Hello Deepika," Raj smiled at her and opened his arms.

"He's proud of you, he loves you, and he knows that you loved him a lot," Anjali spoke up and rubbed Deepika's back tenderly, knowing that there wasn't much she could say to make the situation better.

"I just – I can't even process this…" Deepika trailed off, choking on her words, "It didn't feel real before this. But now…"

She turned to look at the casket next to her and placed one hand on the pristine surface.

"Let yourself feel everything, Deepika," Anjali took the young girl into her arms and hugged her, "And I'm sure you know this, but your father would be disappointed if you stopped celebrating life. Your life isn't over, beta. I know it feels like it, but your father would want you to feel everything and remember him for everything he was. Keep the memories close to your heart, always."

Deepika knew Aunty was right. If Jitendra could tell her one last thing, she knew it would be just that. To love him and remember him, but to never stop living. *Life's too short to worry about tomorrow. Be here, today.* He'd said that on so many occasions, and sometimes it frustrated her to think that he didn't care enough about the future. But deep down, she knew that she had to take the good part of what he believed and stay true to that because that's what he'd want.

At some point, Deepika couldn't cry anymore. She was too fatigued and even though the pain was still gnawing at her, it wasn't eating her alive any longer. Many people came to pay their respects to her and her family. She knew most of them, but she did appreciate the unfamiliar faces that still felt the need to give their condolences to her. Some of those people shared short stories about her dad that she didn't know about and elicited laughter that she was so grateful for, considering the day had been dreadful and depressing overall. In the middle of a conversation her mom was having with her two aunts outside, her phone rang. She'd left it on because William told her he would call before the ceremony was over. Her spirits rose when she saw that it was him on the caller display.

"Excuse me," she glanced at her mother, who knew it was William calling, and said, "I'll be back for the speeches in ten minutes."

Deepika wasn't giving a speech. She was playing music. She felt it was more fitting because her father didn't care for speeches. Although she had so much to say about him, she could share it with close family at home. Even though she didn't believe in the after life or any of that *religious nonsense* as her atheist father would put it, if there was a minute chance that he was watching, she'd like him to hear her play not ramble on about his good qualities.

"Hey baby, how are you doing?" William's voice was soothing on the other end even though he wasn't with her.

Deepika sighed happily, thankful that he had called, and replied, "It's overwhelming, William. I feel this permanent tightness around my neck and in my chest, and I wish it would just go away."

"Hey," William whispered because he hated it when his girlfriend was in pain and he couldn't be there to support her.

"Just..." Deepika felt her eyes well up again, "I just need you to hold me."

Silence. He wanted to as well. He wanted to be there with her at this moment, but his grandfather had passed that morning. He wasn't going to tell her until later on. It was one thing to lose someone who had had a full wonderful life, but it was much more devastating to lose a parent who had his life cut short. William was upset, but he didn't feel that same grief that Deepika felt, so he kept the bad news to himself.

"I will, sweetheart. I'm going to see you soon," William gripped his cell tighter and said, "You're a fighter, Deepika. You're going to make it through this, and I'm going to be with you every step of the way. Go play that Clapton song for him."

"I love you, Will," Deepika was smiling now. He always knew what to say to get to her, and it was because he meant it that she loved him.

"Je t'aime, mon amour. Reste forte." *Stay strong.*

Stay stronger than him is what Deepika heard. That's what he would've wanted too. If his daughter was better than him, then he had succeeded as a parent. Deepika proceeded to the front of the reception hall while Jitendra's friends and family filled the seats. She sat on a chair next to his body and tested her guitar as the guests' low murmurs turned to complete quiet.

"For those of you who don't know," Deepika addressed the audience using the microphone in front of her, "my father played a huge role in making music a large part of my life, and I am forever grateful for that. And I know that we're all sad and heartbroken, but truthfully, he wouldn't want us to be. He would want us to be singing, dancing, drinking, and eating. He would want all of us to celebrate him, not mourn him. As much as I'd like to, I know we also need time to grieve this loss. My father wasn't a fan of speeches, and he didn't differentiate between wedding and funeral speeches either. They both kinda sucked."

Deepika gave the audience a slight smile when she heard some chuckles at her comment. She continued when it got quiet again, "So I thought I'd honour him by doing what he'd really appreciate."

She strummed a chord on her guitar once and looked up and said, "Thank you for making sure I didn't quit, Dad. I'll never stop playing, I hope you can hear the music wherever you are," before she played an instrumental version of Eric Clapton's "Tears in Heaven" for her father.

After the funeral, the days turned to months and things got easier. William eventually told Deepika that his grandfather had passed away, and Deepika had taken the train to Quebec City to be certain he was coping. They were making the distance work, but William had to leave his part-time studies at U of T because his family needed him there for a few months.

Deepika missed her father on certain days more than others. When she had to give her thesis presentation and he wasn't there, she felt his absence. When she was awarded a medal from the Dean for her extracurricular work and high academic standing and he wasn't cheering in the audience, she felt his absence. As the time went by, she began to focus on the people who *were* there. Her mother, Juanita, who had finally returned from an incredible time in France (with a French girlfriend too!), her program friends, Dr. P. After February, the months just flew by, and before she knew it, she was handing in her last final exam of undergrad. When she had come home after that exam, she had been surprised to find all three of her grandparents and both her aunts, who had flown back from India for her graduation, and her mother, with a ridiculously large mint chocolate chip ice cream cake ready to cut to celebrate the end of her final year. Before she could cut into the cake, she heard a familiar husky voice behind her, "You forgot the candles."

She leapt into the air in excitement, forgetting about the knife in her hand, and was about to throw her arms around William when he pointed at the knife and laughed, "You're trying to kill me, already? We aren't even married yet!" The house erupted in a fit of laughter both at his joke and the fact that a crimson-faced Deepika hastily placed the knife on the table and mumbled a quick sorry before running into his open arms.

"How long are you here for this time?" she whispered into his ear.

"Quite a while," he grinned at her when he saw her eyes light up, and then added with a wink, "So don't get any plans to seduce a boring Torontonian!" This time, she laughed with the others. He knew how to light up a room. Her mother had once told her that she did too. Maybe that's how they found each other. The family spent the rest of the night chatting about Deepika's plans for postgraduate studies, the novel she had begun to write, and her plans for the summer. At some point in the evening, after the elders had gone to bed, Juanita showed up with a bottle of sparkling champagne, which they popped in the backyard and drank to each of their successes.

"So...how's Geneviève?" Deepika waggled her eyebrows and teased her best friend after the three of them had settled down on the patio.

William laughed at Deepika's expression and looked at Juanita, who was ready with a witty, and incredibly dirty reply, as usually.

"Oh, she's great...I mean like *really great*," Juanita winked at the couple so that any doubt regarding her insinuation was cleared.

Deepika burst into a fit of laughter and added, "Well, I mean I hear the French are well-versed in a variety of things. Rumours, you know?"

William chuckled, "Oh really..."

Deepika shrugged her shoulders, finding it impossible to hide the smile that crept onto her lips, "I mean, I wouldn't know."

"Oh, you're terrible!" William laughed, kissing her cheek softly.

"Okay but seriously," Deepika started after they'd stopped messing around, "I'm so happy for you, Cruz." She looked at her best friend and got out of her chair to give her a hug.

"Thanks, Dee. Honestly, she's a great girl, and you won't believe it but my parents actually like her."

"No way!" Deepika exclaimed, knowing how disappointed Juanita's parents had been when she'd revealed her sexuality to them a year ago, "That's amazing!"

"I know. Now, there's only one thing left to do," Juanita smiled, as she poured the last round of glasses for her friends.

"What's that?" Deepika asked, as she looked at her friend.

Juanita punched her best friend's shoulder playfully and exclaimed, "Graduate, of course!"

The three of them laughed at the obviousness of that statement and stayed up until an ungodly hour – no one was keeping track of the time that night – joking around and discussing some of Juanita's insanely hilarious experiences in France. They went to bed with happy hearts, dreaming of all the possibilities summer would hold.

Chapter 9

May 12, 2017. Today was the day Deepika had been waiting for. Today she would walk across that stage, get her thirty seconds of glory, and graduate. Four years of hard work finally coming to a close never felt so exhilarating. Deepika tried to calm down as she applied a light shade of lipstick, so that she wouldn't sweat and look like a mess at one of the most important ceremonies of her life. She kept her outfit simple – a beige-coloured A-line dress, a silver watch, and the necklace her father had brought back for her from India on one of his trips there. She wanted to make sure he was there in some form, even if she didn't see him in the audience.

"Can I come in?" Asha peeped through the crack of Deepika's bedroom door as she knocked. She had Jitendra's letter in her hand, finally feeling that the time was right for her to pass it on to her daughter. She hadn't tampered with it or tried to read the contents. While she was curious as to what Jitendra had written, part of her already knew what he would have wanted to tell Deepika. Deepika turned around, stunning her mother with how grown-up and gorgeous she looked. She smiled and told her mother that it was fine to come in.

"Wow," Asha was speechless, but collected herself and said, "You look beautiful, Deepika."

Deepika smiled, "Thanks, Mom."

"Wow, I just can't believe you're graduating," Asha couldn't help the solitary tear that escaped her right eye, but she held it together and continued, "I know it feels like something's missing because Dad isn't here physically. But, he wanted to be here." She pulled the envelope from her jacket pocket and watched Deepika's eyes well up with tears. The first thought she had was a horrific one – had he known that he wouldn't be there for her graduation?

"I know what you're thinking, Dee," Asha comforted her daughter, "But, no, I don't think he had planned anything of the sort. I think he was going to give this to you in person had he been around. You know how he was with verbal displays of affection."

Deepika smiled, remembering how difficult it was for him, and the fact that he'd taken the time to write it all down was extremely touching. If only he had been there to hand it to her himself.

"We don't have to head out for another hour," Asha smiled, "But you don't have to read it now if you don't want to. It's entirely up to you."

Deepika took the letter from her mother and nodded slowly just before her mother left the room to give her daughter some privacy. The envelope felt heavy in her hands, as though as Jitendra had written each word, a fraction of the weight on his shoulders had transferred itself onto the page. She sat by the window of her room with the letter on her desk. Part of her didn't want to read it yet because once it was opened, that was the last thing she'd ever receive from him. The other part of her didn't think she could hold onto the sealed envelope forever because she knew that he'd wanted to tell her something important, and that whatever it was, he'd wanted her to know it today. She was about to go through with it when her phone rang, so she took her friend's call before doing so.

Meanwhile, in the living room, Indu Kaur was sitting with her daughter and beaming at Deepika's achievements. She had been updated over the phone and through mail, but it was an entirely different experience to see the certificates, the transcripts, and the plaques her granddaughter had been awarded over the years for all her work.

"She loves what she's studying," Asha smiled when her mother asked if she wasn't simply working hard for the sake of the grades or her parents.

Indu nodded, squeezing her daughter's shoulder affectionately, and said, "I knew you'd let her find her way."

Asha thought back to her father's note to her after he had died. *Follow your heart*, he had written. It wasn't that he hadn't wanted her to do that from the start, but he'd been a practical man. He'd wanted her to be able to follow her heart and still be comfortable and secure. Perhaps what he hadn't considered was how far genuine dedication could take you because when Asha looked at Deepika's accomplishments in school, she had no doubt that her daughter would carry that forward once she was out. Sure, she thought, pure passion may not get you that far. But passion combined with commitment, drive, and relentlessness – now that, that could do wonders.

Asha sighed happily, resting her head on her mother's shoulder, and said, "You know, despite the horrendous circumstances, I'm glad you're here. It's been ages since you've visited."

Indu held her daughter's hand and replied, "I'm sorry you had to go through that twice."

"There's nothing anyone could have done for either of them," Asha spoke softly, "They were suffering their own internal Hells." She was done with feeling guilty or feeling as though she hadn't done enough. All she had ever tried to do with Jeet was to extinguish the burning flames in his soul and show him that the past only consumed you if you let it. There was so much better to look forward to, so much love around him, but he hadn't been able to embrace it entirely. He'd been stuck and he'd refused to budge, so it hadn't mattered how hard they'd try to push him.

"You're right," Indu smiled for a moment and then became serious, "But I have to warn you, beta, it never fully goes away. It's been years since Kartik crashed his car by the underpass near our home, and every time I drive past it, the memory flashes in my mind. There's nothing I can do about it, but I keep driving. Sometimes I drive straight past it, others I take the riskier route and drive right through the dark tunnel, but I never stop. I promise you that it'll get easier one day, and I know you're going to be fine, Ash. You're going to be fine because you've always lived for yourself first, you're going to be fine because you have an amazing daughter who loves you, and you are the strongest woman I know."

Asha hugged her mother, "The only reason I am this strong is because of you." Indu held her daughter by the fire while they waited for everyone else to get ready. It didn't matter that Asha was nearing fifty. Indu would always see her as the spunky young woman who wouldn't take anyone's nonsense and stood up for what was right, but at the end of the day, would always need her mother.

Deepika had finally opened the envelope and had the letter between her thumb and index finger as she read it so that her other hand was free to wipe away the tears that she had known would inevitably follow. Her eyes took in every word completely as she took her time to read.

Dear Deepika,

I don't consider myself a writer. Sometimes I try, but I know I'm not nearly as good as you, so you may ask, why bother trying? Well, it turns out that I can write better than I can speak in certain instances, like this one. You are graduating today, and I can't be prouder. You are an intelligent, charming, and righteous young woman, and I owe a lot of that to your mother. I am sorry for putting you through so much grief and pain. I am sorry that I don't know how else to be, and I want to tell you that I do hear you. I hear you when you tell me that you care, and that's why you're upset, and I am sorry that I am unable to respond. But enough about that, the reason I am writing this is not to wish you the best of luck because you don't need it. Your academic abilities are beyond me, quite literally. I am always intrigued by your analyses of Camus, Sartre, and even Molière – although, I can't understand French for my life. Your song-writing and poetry skills are brilliant. Yes, I do read your blog links that you post on Facebook from time to time, and yes, I do listen to the lyrics you sing when you're in your room practicing. Although, maybe find a professional singer!

Deepika stopped reading for a second to grab a tissue and dab her wet eyes. She let out a brief laugh at the last line, but the tears kept flowing because she had had no idea that her father had paid so much attention to her. She was eager to know what else he'd wanted to tell her, so she picked the letter up again and continued.

You are a hard-working and well-read young woman – that is why I feel no need to wish you luck. I have no doubt in my mind that you are going to be successful in your career, relationships, and personal goals. Keep being yourself, and you will attract even more light into your life, with the same intensity as the one that emanates from you. Promise me one more thing. Promise me that you won't give up on your goals, just like you never gave up on me.

Love,
Dad

P.S. The Range Rover is yours now. I am thinking of a Porsche for myself. Congratulations!

Deepika was overcome with so much emotion that the words had begun to blur. She laughed through tears at her father's afterthought because honestly, he probably would have gotten his Porsche had he been alive, and then they'd have gotten into a stupid fight over it, but it would've all been fine eventually and they'd be enjoying rides in it a couple of weeks later because staying angry was not Deepika or Asha's strong suit. She then realized that he had had the intention of coming home eventually. He hadn't planned on poisoning himself. That reassurance made her feel better because it told her that he had loved his family enough to want to live.

"Hey," Asha entered Deepika's room quietly, certain that her daughter was overwhelmed.

"I needed to read that," Deepika responded, her tears no longer streaming down her face. She grasped the necklace she was wearing in her fist and closed her eyes, but she was smiling now. She turned to her mother and said, "You can read it if you want to."

Asha was happy to see that whatever Jitendra had written had given her daughter some sense of closure and comfort, so she nodded and said she'd read it after the ceremony but that they had to leave now.

"Before we go," Asha began, pulling out a black box from her purse, "Happy graduation, Dee." She held out the box, and she saw that Deepika had already figured out what it was.

"Holy shit!" Deepika exclaimed, and then quickly covered her mouth and mumbled a sorry for cursing. Asha just laughed at her daughter's excitement because it mirrored how she had felt when she'd received the same gift. Before opening the box, Deepika beamed at her mother and asked, "Is this seriously a Parker 75?!"

Asha was grinning and nodded, "Open it."

Deepika didn't waste another second. She flipped the box open and admired the sterling silver fountain pen. It wasn't enough to just look at it, so she held it between her fingers twirled it in her hand. *Oh god, now I just want to write,* she thought, absolutely ecstatic that this was hers.

"You don't particularly feel like going to grad now, do you?" Asha chuckled at her daughter's marvelling at the high-end writing device.

"Nope!" Deepika laughed, wanting to run to her desk and use the pen. She could sit there for hours with a ballpoint; she imagined she'd be there for days with this gorgeous instrument. Deepika hugged her mother and cried, "Thank you! Thank you! I can't wait to use it – it's so beautiful."

"You're welcome," Asha smiled, and added, "But save the writing for after you graduate!"

With that, they hurried downstairs to find that everyone was ready. William had arrived with Juanita just minutes ago, both of them looking wonderful. Asha took her mother and parents-in-law in her Volvo, and Deepika tossed William the keys to her Range Rover and winked at him before saying, "You drive." She knew he loved driving the SUV nearly as much as her, so she giggled when his face lit up as he caught the keys in his hands. They reached Con Hall in half an hour with enough time to take photos around campus. Asha captured shots with *the trio* – that's the term Juanita had come up with after refusing to be referred to as the third wheel – and the family.

Before she knew it, the Dean had called Deepika's name and she'd stood up to walk across the stage. She shook the Dean's hand and turned to smile at the audience. She saw her family there, and her face fell slightly when she didn't see her father with the rest of them. Glancing at her feet momentarily, she knew she had to be stronger, so she looked straight ahead and raised her diploma over her head and cheered. And for a moment, she saw her dad standing in the aisle, donning a distinguished grey suit and the biggest grin she'd ever seen, cheering for her and clapping louder than anyone in the crowd. She looked directly at him and tipped her diploma in his direction and smiled, telling him that this one was for him. It was barely a minute that she'd been on the stage, but she walked across it and headed back to her seat.

She looked to the aisle once more to see that her father was no longer there, but she didn't let her smile falter because she had done it. She had walked right through the underpass that her grandfather had not been able to pass through, the one that her father had not reached in time for him to get home, the one her grandmother didn't pause to think about any longer. She'd seen the darkness and she refused to let it consume her or force her towards an alternate route. Instead, she had looked directly into it and lit up the nothingness with her presence. And then, she simply walked through it with her head held high and her unrelenting determination.

She didn't stop to look at the dirty writing on the walls, the negative commentary, or the discernable discouragement. She strode forward, not thinking to look back, and saw a glimmer of light on the other side. Approaching it confidently, she emerged with a greater sense of self than ever before, and with her she saw her best friend, lover, and family. They had been walking with her the entire time, and while a few got lost along the journey, they'd been there for her in their own ways. Before Deepika could sit back down, she caught her mother's eye and smiled.

THE END

Manufactured by Amazon.ca
Bolton, ON